CELLO

AND

OTHER STORIES

CELLO

AND
OTHER STORIES

FRANCES THIMANN

Published by
Pewter Rose Press
17 Mellors Rd,
West Bridgford
Nottingham, NG2 6EY
United Kingdom
www.pewter-rose-press.com

First published in Great Britain 2008

ISBN 978-0-9560053-0-4

British Library Cataloguing in Publication Data
A catalogue record for this book is available from the British Library

Cover design by www.thedesigndepot.co.uk

Printed and bound by TJ International Ltd, Padstow, Cornwall

Pewter Rose Press
www.pewter-rose-press.com

CONTENTS

ACKNOWLEDGEMENTS

The collection is based upon some of the stories that I worked on while attending the MA course in Creative Writing at Nottingham Trent University, and I should like to acknowledge the help and support of staff and other students during that time. I should also like to thank all those who form part of a writing group established then, which still continues, and whose members' advice and comments have been invaluable. Lastly, but most important, I must mention Anne McDonnell of Pewter Rose Press for her knowledgeable and tactful support throughout, and for her initiative in suggesting and enabling this publication.

FOREWORD

'Cello and Other Stories' is a collection of short stories about old age and the elderly.

I feel that old people in modern fiction and in the media get a raw deal. Often they are shown as comic, physically disabled, forgetful, or else the victims of neglect and abuse in hospitals and homes. Alternatively they are portrayed as guilt-inducing burdens to their children, their communities, even themselves.

Old age is an 'undiscovered country', and one that no-one is particularly anxious to explore. We are ignorant and afraid of it, and so caricatures and stereotypes are what the subject tends to receive. It is certainly a complex topic, and it is harder to portray the feelings and emotions of the old than the love between younger people, which has always been one of the main themes of literature.

But these days there is a growing body of writing about disadvantaged groups and excluded voices, and I think that the time is ripe for a more positive exploration of the subject. The old have had a lifetime of experience, of happiness and loss, and I hope in these stories to provide some sympathetic images, and to show that even the sad events the elderly may live through can have meaning and importance.

Some of the stories in the collection show older

people still leading significant lives, taking decisions which profoundly affect others; some focus on old people looking back, reflecting in various ways upon what they remember. Others concern younger people and their relationships or encounters with older ones — young people often see their elders distantly, as if through the wrong end of a telescope, not really understanding them. And two of the stories concern people who in their middle years take decisions — or have decisions forced upon them — which dictate the shape of the rest of their lives.

The stories encompass a number of other themes, for example that of cloth or texture, because the fabric of family and community is important to the old, their lives are a weave of memory, history, custom, possessions, and many other things. The importance of documents, letters, notes, and photographs, acting as gateways to and illumination of the past, but sometimes confusing it, is another theme.

Music is a recurring idea, significant in its portrayal of emotion, and its capacity to unite and reconcile, to bring resolution.

I have tried to provide a variety of angles and points of view, and I hope that the collection may go some way towards showing that the subject is full of interest, beauty, and complexity.

MIRIAM

Each quiet day passes; each letter is read once more and laid aside, each old photograph presents its small, four-cornered world of time and place, cut from the long past. Memories become clearer and more coherent, they are pieced together, and understanding moves like late sunlight across the lawn.

My mother had always been beautiful. A picture of her as a young woman, just before her marriage, shows a slight form with perfect, delicate features, short hair squarely cut, in the style of the time. Perhaps it is only the damaged surface of the snapshot, but her skin seems darker here than in reality it was: almost Mediterranean, a Pre-Raphaelite heroine maybe. Her eyes seem to look a little apart, as if recently alerted to something of wider import, or to take in more of the world than was permitted by the conventions of her day.

Even as an old lady, the deep intensity of her eyes was not faded nor lessened, enhanced by the cloudy cotton-white of her hair.

* * *

These days, perhaps, families do not record their lives in this way. I do not know if modern

1

ways are better, but for me there was some comfort, some enchantment even in those forgotten, fading photographs. I was very tired after all that had happened during the last days, but I could not sleep. I sat that evening in my mother's little study with the albums strewn about me, and the stiff covers opened to the past.

I believed that somehow, by searching through these images of her life, I might become closer to her. I hoped that even now, at this late time, I might understand her more clearly, without the unhappiness that had occurred so often between us through the years.

And as I searched through the old albums, I thought of those hours in the hospital again, those few hours by her bedside that had seemed so long. In my mind they became mingled with all the years of my mother's life, made visible in the pictures before me.

"Mrs Stephen? Would you come this way please? You've had a difficult journey, I expect, such dreadful weather, it has come on so suddenly ..."

Yes — here was one that I remembered still, a very early one: my mother, Miriam, as a baby, lying on her mother's lap in long elaborate clothing, exotic like a pagan princess glimpsed in some old travel book. Her face was small and dark, intense even then. She was the youngest child of five, the only girl, and several years younger than her brothers, very much loved. Already as a baby she was beautiful, as a young girl she would have become used to receiving admiration. I looked at the image for a long time; that early likeness explained so much to me. There were many others, simple family records — my mother in a great old-fashioned pram like a Viking ship sailing across a modest suburban garden; unforgiving school uniforms as she grew up, harsh haircuts. Family groups in porches in out-dated clothes, hats like acorns; on beaches in flapping absurd bathing costumes.

The call from the hospital had come early, far too early, a blade of sound that cut sleep painfully away from me. I dressed in the darkness, tumbling down the lowest stairs over last night's shoes. My old car, left outside in last night's cold, would not start, and I waited many hours for the repair. Snow drove forwards, backwards, sideways, a winter's season, fog, wind, and rain in one.

Going to work, her first day perhaps, a secretary in the family firm. A plain winter coat and a beret, topped with its rakish slanted twig, as if she might be lifted up and placed in a more enticing world. She faces the camera, and the adventure of earning her living: excited, calm.

I put the album down for a moment. I wondered what she might have wanted from her life then. Her family had been modest, they could not afford an education for her. For most women at that time there was no prospect of excitement or fulfilment, only marriage and maternity. Her working life would be short-lived, often dull.

Did she find fulfilment or excitement with my father, with her children?

The young nurse led me along the ward. The winter light had found its way here too, heavy as lead. "Your mother is asleep now," she said, looking back at me over her shoulder as she walked. "But she was asking for you earlier, asking if you had come yet. She was hoping she would see you just as soon as you came into the ward."

Perhaps I had not arrived soon enough. Perhaps I had failed her again.

I took up the second album. I found a likeness of my father as her suitor, bespectacled and plain even as a young man, soon to be a professor. She would have respected his knowledge, his scholarship. A studio portrait of Miriam on her engagement, lovely as a film star, but innocent, without glamour or self-awareness. A folder of their wedding photos, my father appearing nervous and uncomfortable, finding himself for once a centre of attention. My mother radiant, her long slender-fitting dress circling suddenly wide and full about her feet, as if showing the fulfilment that a bride should find in marriage.

The young mother with her new baby, joy cut deep and dark in every line and angle of her face: my sister Linda, lovely like my mother. The ideal family, mother, father, child — is this what she desired? And then my own arrival, a baby far less pretty than my sister, sometimes ailing and difficult. Did Miriam realise for the first time, with this second child, that domestic life might become a trap?

I sat by the bedside, the chair awkward and comfortless. Maybe no-one was expected to remain there for long. The curtain that hung crookedly around the bed, and the grey light that hung over the ward became the background to memories of my mother through all our years; years in which my love for her seemed always greater than hers for me. Often in my childhood, I would look up to see those dark, Mediterranean eyes upon me with an expression in their depth that I could not understand. It was as if I were a puzzle for her, had found my way by mistake somehow into her home.

She was a dutiful mother: grazed knees, sore throats, the everyday childhood ailments were always carefully dealt with. But the grazes and ailments of adulthood are not so easily healed. I wondered if she found me less appealing than my sister Linda, always a bright, sweet-natured child, easy to love. Maybe, after Linda, she had hoped for a son. Or maybe her concern for my frail father took all her energy — throughout the years she looked after him with single-minded duty and devotion.

Perhaps merely she did not care for me. Perhaps, perhaps ...

My father, crumpled as always, holding me to his shoulder; an informal snapshot, neither of us looking towards the camera.

But after a time, our parents' presence in the photographs diminishes. My sister and myself, heroic toddlers taking our first brave steps, small legs outstretched as if to walk the plank, no less adventurous than any blindfold pirate. Then as children becoming recognisable, becoming gradually ourselves, coming forward to meet the backward process of memory. Linda and myself again, cat-slim and puppy-fat, in a further procession of school uniforms — strange the things that do not change. Old-fashioned bucket and spade holidays, family cricket on the sands, taking shelter from the wind beneath rocks, wild hair blown over brave smiles.

Was she happy enough at last, as housewife and mother? Or did she dislike the buckets and spades, the upheavals of family life, the glooms of teenagers? But as with so many women of that time, she had no choice, only duty, the only choice then to do it willingly, or not. I had always admired in her the capacity to seem content with very little.

When Linda and I left home at last, she returned to work for a few years. My father told me once that she would sing about the house again, as she had done in the early years of their marriage. She had a sweet voice, but I hardly heard it during the time that we were growing up. She did not listen much to music, it appeared to give her no especial pleasure. Once, I had thought of studying music, becoming a professional player, but she dissuaded me.

Outside, snow swept past the hospital windows still; inside, a few late visitors came and went. Later, trolleys passed with last orders — water, pills, tea. I closed my eyes, listening to soft footsteps, muffled voices, the murmur of electronic instruments. It was almost comforting, as if these were the most important sounds. If a frail life were to slip quietly beneath their surface, it would be of no significance — these were the things that would continue.

"A cup of tea, Mrs Stephen?"

Someone appeared before me in the darkness. A few snowflakes drifted by the window, uncertain of their route.

The last album: relatives, visitors. My father's mother, Charlotte, so like him, but almost blind now in this picture. She had stayed with us often. She had been suddenly and early widowed, left with four children. And here is a very old snapshot, indefinably foreign, out of place surely amongst these domestic ones — my father's family, also a large one, of European origin, artists, musicians, and academics, their lives terribly shaken by the Second World War. They had many Jewish friends. A cousin of my father's, Leon. At the start of the war he was a refugee from central Europe, Vienna I believe. Like many artists and musicians, he found that his work became impossible at that time. He stayed with my newly-married parents for a year before leaving for the wider horizons of the USA. I was not born then, my sister was still a baby. Sometimes, as I grew older, I wondered about those times, and why my parents had spoken to me so little about them. My father occasionally recalled the foreign phrases that Leon had used; my mother, for whom it must have been a harder thing entirely, said nothing. With her simple background, how could she relate to this strange, exotic figure with his tragic history, suddenly become a part of her own small family, disturbing its symmetry?

I wondered for the first time now where Leon might be, and I hoped that he might have a family of his own.

In all those pictures of my father's relatives, I noticed for the first time their strong likeness — some families are like, some not at all. In my own, I realised, we were all different in our appearance, as if we were hardly related. I was quite unlike my mother, though I resembled my father in many ways, my sister not at all.

I wondered if resemblance, or its opposite, affects the way that families connect with one another. Does likeness bring closer ties?

And I wondered again about what might have held my parents together during all the years. I realise now, of course, that most families have their problems. I married too young, looking for those things that my childhood had not given me, and I live apart from Jon now, though one day, I hope, we will find a way to be together. Was my parents' marriage the attraction of opposites, as individuals, and as families? Was their relationship already under strain when I was born? Was her chill towards me the result of the difficulties she felt then? Was her sense of duty, always so strong, all that held her marriage and her family together at that time?

As I looked through all the pictures of the past, I realised how little I knew of my parents' lives, of the lives they had lived before I was born.

"Mrs Stephen? I am Dr Mahmoud." I started, though he had spoken very quietly. I had slept for a while, maybe.

"I am sorry, Mrs Stephen, there is very little that we can do for her."

He checked drips, charts, pulse, a file of notes, his neat slight fingers adjusting her life. He seemed more concerned with these records than with the emptied, motionless figure on the bed. After a time he said: "There has been no history of heart trouble, that is so? Your mother is seventy-four, these days that is young. There has been some sudden shock or strain in these last few weeks? — an unexpected bereavement?"

"Oh, no — no, Dr Mahmoud, there was nothing ..."

"I am so sorry."

He slipped away, no doubt to another bedside.

A few late snapshots, not yet mounted into the album. My mother as an old lady, on her own, more beautiful than ever, the fine lines of her bones more marked in age. Her eyes were intense still, though one was by this time unseeing, as dark within as its outward appearance. The picture recalled that first one of her as a baby, though now she is at the furthest end of her life. She seems as calm, facing her last journey, as determined, as when she set out all those years ago, to her first place of work. She looks at the camera again: serene, fulfilled.

I leant back and closed my eyes for a moment, and I wondered what could be the source of this serenity. Was it only the knowledge of duty done? I had never considered this question, one thinks of these things only when it is too late. Our parents are, for most of our lives, too close, so that we cannot see them clearly.

There was a movement suddenly, and my mother tried to raise herself a little. She seemed to notice me for the first time, although her eyes were quite sightless. To my astonishment, she stretched her hand and touched mine, covering it with greater warmth than I could ever remember. She prepared herself to say something to me, she worked hard to speak, but I could hear only a few of the words, and they made no sense:

"… at last … Lucy … we — your father … oh my dearest …"

I stood at the study window, drew back the curtains. The snow had stopped earlier in the day, and lay quiet and expectant over street and garden.

At the very bottom of the cupboard, beneath all the letters and albums, I found a small folder, differently shaped, flat. Some papers wrapped in tissue, fragile like aged skin. Writing in my mother's hand, some in a hand I did not know. Very tired by this time, but feeling that I must continue the task until the end, I undid the ribbon and looked at what was within.

I drew out old sheets of music, yellowing and crumbled at the edges, the fretted coastline of a strange country: inlets, bays, sharp creeks. The notes, hand-written, black and firm, very clear still. A song: the text written beneath it, a piano accompaniment. I looked at the words. It was a love song; at the top, a dedication, a woman's name simply — my mother's.

Then the composer's name.

Below that, another song, a gentle lullaby, a dedication at the top: 'To An Unknown Child'. I read the music, it was full of longing and love, written, strangely, for a man's voice alone, without accompaniment. There was something of Central or Eastern Europe in the angles of its melody. The composer's name.

It was three in the morning.

I opened the old family piano — perhaps he had played it too. It was out of tune now, the pedal groaning. I lit candles upon it, and I played the songs that my father had written, songs to the woman he loved and could not marry, and to their child, whom he could never know nor see.

* * *

Letters …

My mother's solicitor wrote, in his stiff, dry tone, of the events surrounding Leon's arrival and stay in this country — there was little by that time that I did not know or could not guess. My eyes slipped over his words, until the final phrases:

> *… Leon Hecht died suddenly, a few weeks ago, aged about eighty, I understand, an event which I believe may have hastened your mother's final illness.*
>
> *Your parents had agreed that when Leon died, but not until then, you should be told the identity of your true father, if by that time Robert Hecht was also deceased. Your parents also agreed that Leon's estate*

should be left to you entirely, as he has no remaining family now, nor heirs.

Your mother requested me to ensure that all correspondence, jewellery and gifts given to her by Leon during the course of their relationship, which she placed recently in my keeping, should be passed to you in due course.

I enclose a letter from your mother addressed directly to you, which she asked me to forward at the appropriate time.

And after a moment I opened the letter that my mother had written to me. The form of the music cannot become clear until the last notes have been heard.

AMBER

As he searched for his keys, his fingers touched the stones in the soft wrap that he had found for them — he'd forgotten they were there. The keys were below them, half-slipped into the small ambitious hole that would soon, he knew, successfully engulf them. Fumbling, he could feel the moist heat of the room again, he saw once more the casual, confident curve of the girl's bright hair, the light shining upon it. He remembered the heavy scent that slipped about her as she moved, leaning towards the boy as a plant leans to entwine about a tree. He wondered who they were, and if they could understand — if they were ever to know — what it was that they had done.

* * *

The September evening was warm as he waited, the sky low and close about the narrow roofs, the stunted urban trees. Soon, he thought, the evening would become uncomfortable and oppressive. He was formal and stiff in his unaccustomed suit, raincoat neatly folded, unnecessary, over one arm: a tall man, moving beyond middle age, his hair receding a little from the corners of his forehead. His eyes were very dark, behind old-fashioned, brown-framed glasses — they looked a little apart. His arms were long and angular, the hands and fingers thin, with fine dark hair along the back.

He'd come early, as always, but the small bar of the restaurant was filled already, with young people for the most part. The air was thick with the sour fumes of wine, and with the regular tuneless beat of heavy music like waves against a rock. He'd not been here for years — the whole area had changed, the place had become fashionable, he supposed. It was no longer the comfortable, traditional restaurant that he remembered. Audrey would have preferred a quieter place, he knew, he could imagine the gentle hesitation in her eyes: 'I'm sure it will be very pleasant, Stephen!' she would politely insist. But if only for a moment he found himself wishing that somehow all this was no longer necessary. He looked about him — everywhere he saw young couples, hand-in-hand, arm-in-arm, even mouth-to-mouth, confident and at ease with each other.

He thought of Audrey often these days. He liked to pass, when he could, the old-fashioned shop in the High Street, with its worn, uneven steps leading upwards to the entrance. He'd gone to purchase something pretty for his sister's birthday, and Audrey was there already, with a necklace for repair. He saw her first, small and slightly built, half-turning to see who had entered. The amber stones lay along the counter. As the assistant consulted with a colleague they waited together, and it seemed natural to him to speak to her about them, for he saw that they were good pieces, perhaps valuable.

"May I? ..." he said, smiling at her. "These are very fine."

He took them in his bony fingers, admiring the smoothness of the pieces to the touch, the soft colour, the half-imagined dry fragrance that lingered on his skin. He remembered a collection of the stones he'd seen once in a museum, some pale, almost translucent, others more warmly coloured. Some had tiny creatures preserved within, insects and butterflies, their wings intact still, or fragile petals and leaves, just as they had been when caught there, helpless, by the sticky fluid, so long ago.

A week later he had seen her in church, her face conspicuous amongst the elderly population, softened by a subdued golden glow of candles. Driving home in heavy rain he'd caught sight of her stepping abstractedly through puddles, and stopped to offer her a lift.

"May I? ..." he said, and smiled once again, leaning towards the window. He remembered the quick movement of her brown glove as she wiped moisture from her face, stooping to speak to him. It may have been rain, and the heavy sweep of windscreen wipers muffled her voice. He remembered the wisps of damp hair, escaping from an unflattering scarf.

"It so often seems to be wet on Sundays," she remarked.

Some days later they sat amongst the shadows of a quiet lounge, drinking coffee. One or two other couples there were insubstantial in the dimness, deserted by waiters.

He told her briefly about Catherine. It seemed natural for him to do so, even after so short an acquaintance. For the first time then, he thought, Audrey looked at him for more than a few seconds.

"I am so sorry," she said at last, simply, in her quiet voice, slightly husky, that reminded him of the cloudy fragrant powder that Catherine had used, as if it filled her mouth, her throat as she spoke.

She added, "My father was an invalid too ..." She talked hesitantly about it, as if she had not done so before, and he sensed that it was a relief for her to do so: "... for six years, before he died." She had a way of completing her sentences after a pause, as if the stream of thought had gone underground and wandered a little, to become lost, or to appear again in another place.

"That was almost a year ago, on Christmas Eve," she added slowly, frowning briefly at the irrelevant remembered detail. He saw the fine threads that cut the blue-white skin about her eyes, lines that he had not noticed in the poorly-lit shop. When she smiled, new lines formed above her cheek-bones, about her mouth, as if her skin were some too-fine fabric that held every crease and mark. Her hair was a soft auburn cloud about her face, but perhaps it was not as bright as it had once been. She was like a rose left too long in its vase, he thought, the water gone, so that if it were moved it might flutter away to pink-brown petals and a last fragrance.

She drank a little of her coffee. He saw the tiny, delicate bones at her throat, the softness between, and he looked away sharply, embarrassed, as if he had seen some part of her that he should not. He wondered suddenly if she would like to have children: then he thought that maybe she would not be interested in — those things. It would surely be too late for her.

She told him that her mother had died years ago. Her father had married again, a much younger woman, and there were two boys. "But she left him, she left her boys ... Dad got ill soon after that."

Some music played in the background, something slow, almost static. In the corner an elderly couple flirted. The man was coarse and carrot-fingered, the woman coquettish, with ginger unconvincing hair and heavy make-up.

Her face was a pale impasto, her mouth a gallant pink stripe in its midst. They were incongruous, two sticks trying to flower.

"I was engaged," she said at length, very quietly, as if it were a confession, "... just when it all happened. Peter and I — we were going out to Canada, to live .... He was an engineer — it was a very good job for him." A bright blush as of guilt covered her face, and she dropped her eyes, afraid perhaps to see disapproval in his. "It seems a long time ago now. I — I broke the engagement ... I couldn't leave Dad just then, and Jack and Toby were still at school ..."

The frightened, crazy knot of lines that was her frown appeared again above her small straight nose, disfiguring her face for a moment. She smoothed it involuntarily with a forefinger. Where were Jack and Toby now, he wondered, though he did not ask her.

He recalled her house — she had remained there when her father died — he'd seen it only for a short while. It was large and very shabby. At the front, a swaying fence drunkenly defended a yard of broken stones; at the back, a wild tumultuous garden, hidden from the street. He had envisaged tea-cups and chintz — and the street might once have been genteel. From the hall, he had glimpsed tall flights of stairs, he imagined dull airless landings where the shadows moved.

He found it difficult. He was fifty-four now, conscious of the stooping roundness of his shoulders, the white flowering of hair before his ears. He felt awkward and foolish, wooing a woman as if he were a youngster; he did not know what the rules were. He'd been married late. Catherine, the slight, fair girl whom he had known from his teens became ill soon after their honeymoon, and for twelve years he'd cared for her alone. Every night still, as he tried to sleep, he saw the sad white geometry of her face again, her frightened eyes, the delicate bones of their sockets. He remembered her hair, soft and abundant to the end, as if the youth and loveliness gone from her face and body somehow still remained there. There were no children, of course, and in the final years, desire had hardly troubled him.

He had no family of his own, only a married sister. Sometimes he would read of an old man dead for a week before he was found, and he wondered if one day that would be his own fate. In the evenings, sitting alone in his gloomy flat with his school marking and his textbooks, or listening to music, he could hear the comings and goings of the youngsters in the rooms about him — most of the houses in the decaying road were let to students now. Later, he heard their cries and sighs, uninhibited, and he would frown, unsure if noise or silence were preferable;

turning the music up a little, or forcing himself to sleep.

He touched the package in his pocket. He had bought her a bracelet, earrings, chosen with care, to match the necklace. He liked the warm colour of the stones, it seemed prettier to him than anything brighter or more glamorous.

Beside him on the narrow pavement, the shops were closing, putting out their angular boxes and bags of rubbish; behind him a fly buzzed feebly, imprisoned amongst sweet cakes in a shop window. It was a faint sound that he heard without turning.

"Stephen — you have been waiting, I am so sorry!"

Suddenly she was there, smiling at his abstraction. She wore a bright summer dress that he thought was new, with pink roses and coppery leaves entwined, very light and bright. But it was too bright; she looked older. She'd done something to her hair, for there was a harshness about its colour now that didn't suit her, and in the mild evening light she seemed to have too much make-up on her face. Once more he felt embarrassed, and filled with unease. But he was touched at the effort she had made, and he forgot the unnatural brightness when she looked up at him with a sweetness that could not be spoiled, and with a hope she could not conceal.

He touched her arm in greeting. "Audrey, my dear ..." As they were shown to their table a sudden awkwardness seized them so that at first they hardly knew what to say, where to look. The table was too small, they were too close, the light too bright. It was not the table he had booked, though he had confirmed it again, fussy as ever, he reflected. It was near the kitchen, and waiters hurried by, knocking against them: "Excuse me sir, if you would just move your chair a little ..." The heavy music had followed them in, forceful in their ears. Audrey fussed with her bag, blushing brilliantly. We should be at home, he thought, drinking tea and completing the crossword, comfortable and unromantic in middle age.

As they finished their first course, another couple brushed past with breathless apology and a flurry of bags and keys, taking the table that might have been theirs: a young couple, laughing, excitedly in love. And he hardly knew what happened then, for it was over very quickly. He saw a lovely nakedness of neck and shoulder, a breast, half-revealed. He saw the tilt of her head as the girl smiled up towards the boy, and the slow fall of her hair, almost liquid, glistening under the brilliant orange light. He saw the boy's crimson lips, his sweat; his fingers caressed her throat. As they looked together at the menu they kissed, their mouths working, writhing, twisting deep, slugs in a muddy pool.

The music thrust at their senses, it seemed to surround them, inescapable. Audrey tried to continue with her meal, but her make-up was smudged, her features blurred, and he could not look at her scarlet, coarsened face. At last she put down her fork.

"I — I seem to have a headache", she murmured, without looking at him. "I think I will go home." She rose quickly. Outside he fussed ineffectually about her, gestured at length for a taxi. His dark face was darker with embarrassment, his narrow shoulders pathetic, long limbs distorted. It was very hot.

"Audrey, may I see you again?" he tried to say at last, but it was a hoarse, explosive sound. He could not find her eyes, nor her hand, he could not touch her, though he tried; the muffled whisper that he heard from her was no reply.

* * *

He stood on his rusty balcony an hour later, the line of his body like a question-mark. There was still light, and a scent of flowers from the garden beyond. From an open window he heard the notes of a saxophone, played by one of the students, maybe. The smooth sound swayed about him, melancholy and honey-sweet, an echo of the music he had heard before.

He thought for some reason of Catherine. Ten years ago he would have gone to her room, done for her the tender, intimate things that she needed, kissed her good-night, touching her bone-lined cheeks one last time before going to his own room. Now there was no-one. He would glance at a book maybe, pour a small drink, as he'd done almost every evening for years; and it would be the same now, until the books and the papers rose above his head to stifle him. He would hear the students come laughing and talking up the hall, every year a fresh generation, and the sounds slowly die away again. He thought of Audrey, already in her own home again, mounting the dark stairs, avoiding the rough edges of the carpet, trying not to see the crawling shadows. He heard her uneven breath, saw the lines at her eyes, the harsh unnecessary make-up.

The curved sky seemed to sink more heavily about his narrow shoulders; he could hardly breathe. There was a little light still along the shabby street, sallow and brown — but the view wouldn't change for him now, whichever way he looked.

The stones lay cold and dry in his pocket.

We are creatures in amber, he thought, helpless, caught and held by the past, half-turning towards a future.

'It will pass,' he reflected. 'I'll phone her again soon, in a few days, or send flowers. Or I could write, to reassure her ... Yes, surely it would be better to write ...'

CLOTH OF GOLD

Since he had come to live near his daughter and the family in this quiet part of the town, he preferred to walk this way, through the Park towards the High Street, or to the market at the foot of the hill. He could buy the few things fresh each day that were all he needed for himself now, slipping in some forbidden sweets for little Sarah, perhaps, whenever he could remember ... The Park always seemed to him a gentler, more peaceful world; the air was softer, and the skies were clearer to his fading eyes. At the highest point there was a small lake, almost encircled by quiet trees, and a flower garden, full of scent now in late summer, where he liked to sit and rest sometimes after the shopping. Often he saw squirrels amongst the plants and bushes, making little chains and threads with their darting and leaping, as if they were sewing along the edges of the grass, hemming up the tidy borders.

He fumbled absent-mindedly in his old canvas bag. It had been young Sarah's first small birthday present to him, when he came to live nearby; it seemed not so long ago. 'So you will be able to help us with the shopping,' she had said, with seriousness, conferring an honour, her blue eyes so bright they seemed to smudge her face, and Janey had smiled, a little embarrassed. His fingers were stiff and unsteady, they searched of themselves for something to give the squirrels, for they were tame and would eat from his hand. The two frail bones stood out at the back of his neck as he stooped, beneath the wispy uneven horseshoe of white hair.

The ritual with the squirrels soothed and reassured him. Behind him two children stood watching, waiting, until the little ceremony was completed.

* * *

"Janey love," he whispered, and stooped to embrace her about the shoulders, very gently, for there was so little he could do now without causing her pain. "All right, love?" Conversation seemed artificial to him here, though he tried to keep his voice calm, so that he should not worry or disturb her; but it was hard for him to see his daughter lying motionless and in pain amongst these feeble, grey-faced old women. He noticed that her hair, which had been so bright and fair, was dull now, and her grey eyes, very soft and pretty, were sunken and colourless. She looked older, much older than her thirty-five years. She had always been frail, even as a child, from the difficult birth, and now her frailty had turned to illness and pain. There was no cure, no operation that could help her.

"Not so bad, Tom," she murmured, and he could hardly hear her. "A bit better today, perhaps," and she put out her hand towards him, though otherwise she lay very still.

The ward was pleasant and sunny, full of late, bright, honey-coloured light.

"I've brought a few flowers, look, love," he said. "I'll put them here, so you can see them." And he found a glass and put them to stand in the window. They moved a little with the movement of air. She had always loved flowers, even when she was a little girl, and these were like the bunches he had picked from the fields and brought to Beth, so awkwardly, in the early days, before they were married; it seemed not so long ago.

He sat there quietly, sometimes touching her hand, sometimes rearranging her things clumsily, unnecessarily, smoothing her sheets or pillows, trying to make her more comfortable: not succeeding.

"It's all right, Dad," she muttered, half asleep, dulled with drugs; or "don't fuss, Tom!" with something of her old spirit. He wondered what changes in a person and what remains the same. Sometimes he would try to talk a little of the past, of the time in the old house, the two of them together, for he had Janey to look after, of course, when Beth had died so young, with the second child. Or he would talk of the small everyday events of family life that she so much missed, and she would smile and press his hand. He knew that he never been much of a conversationalist. Often they would remain for an hour or two without speaking together, yet without awkwardness.

"You and Jane never seem to talk much, but you always know what the other one's thinking!" Alan had said once, suddenly, looking over at them both, as they sat with newspaper and sewing. It had not struck him before, but he supposed it was true. They had always been very close.

Once even he fell asleep himself, waking with a start when one of the nurses touched his arm.

"Here you are, Mr Johnson!" she said, well-meaning, very kind, very young. "A cup of tea — you'll feel all the better for a cup of tea."

He had to try to keep things clean by himself now that Janey was ill, following her whispered instructions.

"Under the window, Dad, where they've always been!" she told him, and shook her head a little at his helpless ways, in the way she had.

Recently, sitting in the sunny little kitchen of his home, digging with slow fingers into Janey's old basket of rags and remnants, he found some material at the bottom that felt strange, though his fingers seemed to remember it of themselves. Slowly he pulled it out from the depths of the bag, his thick white brows moving, his mind working to be there before his eyes. Then both were filled at the same time with the brilliant colour, though the stuff was not as bright as it had been, and in places it was threadbare. It was the little jacket he had given Beth, all those years ago, something he had found on his own while away on business, and kept to give to her when he returned. They had not been married long then, but already they were making plans about the family they would have, the extraordinary things they would do, like any young couple.

He remembered his uncertainty, his worry that after all he had made a mistake with it. "I'm not sure if it's right, Beth love," he told her, watching her unwrap the little parcel. "I didn't know what size to tell them, in the shop ..."

"Oh Tom — it's beautiful! ..." she exclaimed at last, her brown eyes excited, surprised perhaps that he should have chosen something so fine. "Wait there just a minute, now!" And she went quickly to slip the blouse on in the other room (even though they were then several months married). He remembered how pretty her hair had been, long and very fair, with the sun on it, from the window. The stuff was silken and shimmering like water; it was slender-fitting, with a high collar, long tight cuffs. Once he had tried to describe the blouse to little Sarah. He had smiled to see the tiny shading in the girl's eyes, the slight movement of her lips, as the thought lodged with difficulty that her grandmother, whom she knew only from photographs, could at any time have been young, had appeared lovely to a man, even only to Grandpa, and very long ago ...

* * *

On a good day, they might start a crossword together, he and Janey, perhaps only a word or two before she tired. He was beginning to look very frail himself, his narrow shoulders becoming more bent, his neat features losing their cohesion amidst the cobweb lines and wrinkles of his face. He was like a child, in the presence of something he did not understand: waiting.

Sometimes Alan would come, on his own, or with Sarah perhaps, and he would leave them together then. He thought of the life they had all had together; it was ending now. Small scenes, especially in the early years, were clear, like reflections on quiet water, long later years vague and often blurred ...

He could remember the day that Janey told him of her engagement. She was only eighteen then, younger even than Beth had been when they were married, very slight and shy. He had sat alone in his room for a while, his knobbed hands restless on his knees, seeking the comforting familiar crease of his trousers. His square heavy shoes were turned up at the toes with age, the threads of his hand-knitted waistcoat uncurling at the neckline. He went at last into the attic and found the chest where he kept Beth's things still, a few old pieces of her jewellery, some photographs. He found the blouse, old-fashioned perhaps, but lovely even now, he thought, and he wrapped it in tissue to give to Janey. He had meant to wait until she was twenty-one, but this seemed to be the right time, after all. They went to a little restaurant together a few days later, the three of them, and Janey wore the blouse that evening.

"Do you like it this way, Dad?" she whispered, looking up at him anxiously. "I had to alter it a bit, it was frayed really badly in the cuffs and collar. I — I'm afraid I had to cut them, I couldn't think what to do ..."

She had always been clever at sewing. Her hair was very fair in the candlelight, fairer even than Beth's had been. Somehow, through all the years, he had not realised how pretty she had grown. She wore the blouse sleeveless, with a low neck, and he thought it was lovelier than ever that way.

They had always been close; but sometimes, as he got older, he found his thoughts of Janey had become all confused with those of Beth. He would say something to her as if she were Beth, and she would look at him strangely. "It's me, Dad!" she would murmur in the way she had, very softly, and touch his hand.

And during all the time he had hardly known or thought what happened to the blouse, until at last he found it that day in the basket. But there were only a few threadbare pieces left now. Janey must have used the best of the stuff for something else, something for young Sarah, maybe. He thought of a little suntop she once had, and the ribbons she sometimes wore in her hair. He sat in the empty, narrow kitchen as the light faded, holding the pieces in his unsteady hands, until they slipped to the floor. He thought back over the years, his head sunk lower on his chest, the cleaning all forgotten.

"You'll be all right, Dad ..." Janey cried out, struggling to rise, looking directly at him, but with small, sightless eyes. He took her strange, weightless hand in his own two for a moment, each finger working to give her life.

* * *

He rested in the garden overlooking the lake once more, tired already after the short walk up the hill. Everything was taking him longer these days, since Janey died. September leaves stirred in the slight breeze, like memories and thoughts disturbed. He sat preoccupied, white wisps of hair hovering about his head. His stiff hands worked a little of themselves, spreading on his knees; the skin of his face was all fallen in amongst the bones.

There was no-one left in the Park by this time, the young mothers with their prams and pushchairs were gone long ago, the children had been called home to supper. He had not noticed their departure. He had not noticed the drift of time about him, as he had hardly felt the drift of the years as they passed.

One day soon, he knew, they would be leaving too, Alan and little Sarah. It was only a matter of time, six months, perhaps a year, before they would be gone. Janey had told him some time ago, before she became ill, that Alan's firm had suggested a posting to London.

"It's an important move for him, Dad — he can't turn it down ..." and her eyes were excited and proud for her husband.

More recently, the boy had muttered, "It'll be good for you to get away after this, Tom ..." He put his hand on the old man's sleeve, his good face full of concern. He would ask again soon,

Sarah too, she would plead with him, her eyes full of brilliant blue tears like sapphires, not understanding. But Alan would marry again one day, there would be a new mother for Sarah. He would not see her as she grew, playing in the garden with the sun in her hair, her eyes becoming bluer every day. He knew he could not move again, part of him was scattered here like the dust on the path. But the flowers seemed to twist in disorder now about the seats and over the fences that were barely able to restrain them, and since Janey died he had seen something ugly in their pinks and purples, their soft textures, their heavy fragrances.

He drew his thoughts together, folding them into his mind as he had folded the cloths in the kitchen at home into the basket. He rose and turned to go. His foot slipped on an uneven stone, and sharp pain cut through his leg. He wondered how long it would be before disability and sickness might take him as they had taken Janey, and Beth before her, and his future stretched before him longer, infinitely longer than all the past.

The sun was low in the sky, more brilliant, the lines between shadow and brightness upon the grass grew stronger. From where he stood he could catch a glimpse of the town a short way away, framed by trees, as if it were floating in the warm evening light. The same light hovered along the surface of the lake, sliding between the graceful branches, dancing and fluttering there like butterflies' wings. Great leaves drifted slowly to the ground about him, he saw everything through a veil of drifting leaves. It was very quiet. As he watched, the sun slipped quickly towards the water, so that for a few moments the surface of the lake shone soft and gold. He thought again of Beth, and of the silk he had given her when they were married; it seemed not so long ago. For a few seconds he could almost see her before him again, with the light in her eyes and the sweetness in her look. 'Oh, Tom — it's *beautiful*! ...' He heard Janey's voice, 'It's me, Dad!' very gentle, and he felt the touch of her hand. But gradually the colour on the water faded, so that there were only circles of pale light, then a few bright threads that glimmered and glittered here and there upon the surface; fading, rising for a moment elsewhere, thinner, and fainter, until all was dark and still.

A wind turned and circled along the path, an old torn bag blew with it. It seemed to herald the dry decay of autumn, the unravelling of the season.

And he thought of the empty windows of his house, the chair by the fire with the newspaper laid upon it, the crossword that nowadays he could not finish; the silent evenings.

Sailing to Zanzibar

20th January, 1990

I think evening must be the loveliest time here. Yesterday, after we arrived and had rested for a while, we walked through the old town to the seashore. There are about twenty of us in the tour group. Beyond the harbour wall the sea rose up to the horizon just like a great peacock's tail, fanning and swaying, turquoise and violet. Along the waterfront the local men were preparing food for the evening meal — the whole town seemed to be gathering there to eat. We watched as they crushed long sugar canes in ancient mangles, squeezing out colourless sweet juice (we tried some, and it was delicious) or fried octopus and squid (we didn't dare try these!) in shallow wide pans, slicing strange-shaped vegetables and fruits into the oil. The scent of wood-smoke and spices drifted round us.

Boys ran shouting and laughing, diving from the wall into the water, and their heads appeared again like currants, bobbing and dipping at the surface. Then the sun seemed to fall, quite suddenly, rather than to set in a calm and sedate fashion, as it does in England. It burned a path downwards to the sea, and somehow it was like a great tragedy that everyone watched, from the shore, or from their balconies, as if it were happening on a wide stage.

The sky was golden and scarlet beyond the palm trees. Far out to sea, a sail appeared at the horizon and turned in to harbour, its spar slanting, moving quickly on the last wind.

Then the colour disappeared all at once, and it was night.

January, 2008

Gwen stands in her narrow hallway, steadying herself for the difficult climb. In the darkness, the familiar surfaces and spaces of the daytime have become a labyrinth of shadows that move unpredictably as wild creatures.

Since her illness, her balance has become unsteady, her sight and her hearing are weaker. Sensations within her body have become confused with those beyond it, so that she feels she is crumbling into the world around her.

With painful fingers she touches the night-time switches once more, the locks and chains and bolts, all the little devices for her safety. She moves slowly along the hall.

24th January, 1990

I chose this place, Zanzibar, from all the others in the brochure, because it sounded so different, so exotic, so far away! And I have decided to keep a diary during my stay here. I've not done this since I was a teenager, since before I became engaged to Bill, all those years ago! — but it's easy to forget, especially as one gets older, and I should like to remember everything that happens during this holiday. It's a wonderful opportunity for me to escape for a while, at least, after all the sadness and worry of these last few months and years.

Now that Bill is gone — and dearest Bill was never fond of travelling! ('I don't want to become discontented, Gwen,' he would say, and I never found a reply to this) — now that he is gone, I have to get used to being on my own. But the other members of the group seem very pleasant.

Even after several days here, we find the labyrinths of the old Stone Town confusing. The narrow lanes twist and turn behind the palaces of the waterfront and the grand houses where the famous explorers of earlier times — Livingstone and Stanley are the best-known, I suppose —

lived and planned their journeys, and where they returned, sick and exhausted, but enduring bravely till journey's end. The Stone Town is crumbling these days, its stained balconies and fading walls are decaying in the humid climate. The gorgeous wooden doors are often split and broken-down, though they are still most striking. The island is famous for these doors, often beautifully carved with foliage and animals, and it's almost as if they are 'magic casements', inviting us to step through to find a better life. But we found them in the poorer streets too, less fine of course, and sometimes there was nothing behind them at all, just damp and dirt and emptiness.

In one of those tumble-down houses, miserable and wretched, we saw three small children playing, all alone, the oldest would have been about six, maybe. I dropped behind the group for a while, thinking that I'd like to speak to them, to reach out and help them in some way, but they stopped their play and stared at me with their large, grave eyes, until I became uncomfortable, and went on.

Later, a little boy ran up to me, very daring.

'Where you from, lady?' he called out. 'You English lady?' Then he ran away again, laughing at his daring, without waiting for my answer.

They are such beautiful children, thin, malnourished I suppose, their knees protruding like match-heads above their skinny calves. It occurred to me that in a way they are like Zanzibar itself. Their eyes and teeth, their ragged shreds of clothes are so brilliant and bright, but their streets and homes are dark and poor.

I thought of my little grandson Joe, pale and polite and serious — already he has everything that he could ever want.

Later we visited a museum, built like a mosque, of pure white stone, and dedicated to the history of Zanzibar. Amongst all the things I saw there, I remember Dr Livingstone's medical bag the most clearly. It was hardly bigger than a handbag, and it held only a few small bottles and rough-looking implements, all that he had with him as he travelled through Africa.

'It's less than anything a modern tourist might take, even for a short holiday in Europe!' I exclaimed to our tour guide, Freddie.

'You're quite right, Gwen,' Freddie remarked, glancing at me as if he had not thought of this before. 'He was a brave man.'

I should have liked more time there. Stupidly, I hadn't realised that the island was connected with the slave trade — I am learning so much here already — but another excursion had been arranged for us in the afternoon. We were taken to see a workshop where local people demonstrated and sold their crafts, and we were able to buy gifts and souvenirs. Perhaps there'll be an opportunity later in the week to visit the museum again.

January, 2008

She struggles up the stairs, as she does each night, setting herself to the task, bent forward, concentrating on each movement. Her old bag is slung around her, shoulder to hip, her stick clicks along the banister-rails. This step creaks, that one has somehow become taller than the others since the previous night; at the curve of the staircase there are new and dangerous loose threads in the carpet. The shadows trick her, and she tries to ignore them — a second's distraction, and she might fall again. The landing is full of sharp corners too, hard-edged furniture, heavy doors and handles — dangerous ground to cross before she can enter the soft safety of her bed. Gwen knows that this is the proving point of her life, that she should not look back, she should not complain. She must go bravely, like the great explorers she had learnt about so many years ago, journeying to the edges of their world without maps or markers.

26th January, 1990

Yesterday was disturbing and strange, it gave me much to think about. In the morning I slipped away from the tour group, and from Freddie. I wanted to see things for myself, to explore the town, for I may not have another opportunity to travel in this way again, at least for a while. I suppose I'm afraid of everything that lies ahead of me, afraid of growing old. My son is married and gone away, and little Joseph is going to school in France now. Sometimes I look after him in the holidays, and I look forward so much to his visits. Of course I hope that one day perhaps they will return for good.

I was searching for an old Turkish bath, which was marked on the map I had found for myself in the local tourist office. It appeared to be in one of the very poorest parts of the town, not much visited by foreigners, and I wondered if it might have been demolished, or crumbled away long ago. Soon I was quite lost, the lane I was following became just a puddled track between empty buildings. Ugly waste land and heaps of rubble lay ahead of me, and a stained brick wall with no way through that I could find. Other ruined buildings mouldered all round me. For once, in this crowded island, there was no-one there, and for that moment I felt very alone, and a long way from home. Everything was different and rather frightening.

Eventually I found a small shop, and the man there gave me directions back to the hotel. Before I went on my way, he pulled out an old wooden chair for me, brushing the dust away with his fingers. I was tired and hot, glad to rest for a little. I felt no anxiety.

He offered me a pale-coloured drink in a smeary glass.

'You drink, please, lady,' he said. 'Is good for refresh. Is from coconut,' and it was sweet and cool.

I sat there for a little, amongst the loose batteries and packets of matches, dented cartons of washing powder and piles of bananas. The man was thin and small, and the skin of his face and hands was like the bark of an old tree, cracked and broken. But his eyes were very kind, and he treated me as if that little shop were his kingdom, and I an Arabian princess, from the 1001 nights, maybe.

I thought afterwards, for some reason, that the man might be about Bill's age, but it was impossible to tell or to compare. And I couldn't help wondering whether Bill would have been so kind, if an exotic lady from Zanzibar had arrived on his doorstep one day, seeking directions!

Of course, I arrived very late for lunch, the others waiting, looking at the clock, and Freddie most annoyed with me, his charm and his smile quite gone, disappeared like the Turkish bath.

'You must not leave the group again, Gwen,' he scolded me. 'We didn't know what had happened to you. There are places here where it's not safe to go alone.'

Freddie is responsible for us all, of course, and I didn't want to upset him again, nor the other members of the group. I sat quietly on the lawn after lunch, under the canopy — the sun is so hot in the afternoons. Suddenly I am missing Bill very much.

Later, in the early evening, we visited a pleasant spot along the coast, where there had once been a Sultan's palace. It had been burned down, now just a few parts of it remain, and it was peaceful there, the ruined buildings surrounded by gardens and palm trees. It was cloudy that day, and the sky was just beginning to lose its colour, but at that moment it was like pearl or opal, ivory and cream and pink, as if all those colours of the palette were melted together, smoothed and softened by the feathery palms. And yet it was so similar to an English country churchyard! I couldn't help feeling that this would be a tranquil resting-place — though when the time comes, of course, I shall be with Bill in our little village at home.

It's strange that one can travel so far, and discover a place that seems at first so very different — the trees and flowers, the buildings, even the air were foreign — but the atmosphere, and the feelings and thoughts I experienced there, were the same as if it had been England.

But it is England that is beginning to feel far away and foreign to me, and I know that it will be damp and cold there now.

January 2008

On the landing Gwen pauses, short of breath, the familiar pain forming around her heart. From the window she sees the winter sky like an iron vault, bare black trees beneath, a colourless string of moon dropped between the branches: small sharp stars, very distant. Sometimes, in her loneliness, she feels that she is standing at the peak of a great mountain range that stretches far into the distance, or that she is becalmed at the centre of a silent sea. Sometimes she feels that time too has become endless, every minute has become an hour or a year.

She feels that she must hold fast to a chair, a door, so that she will not be brushed away.

28th January, 1990

Freddie is keeping an eye on me, I think! — but I don't have any wish to explore again on my own just now, I am glad to rest for the moment. The hotel is air-conditioned, not hot or humid, and it's situated almost on the beach, so that I can sit and look through the window at the sea as I have breakfast. Fishermen go by, and I saw an old woman returning home with the goods she had bought at the market, all stuffed together into an old string bag, a wretched chicken squirming at the bottom beneath all the cans and tins. Tomorrow there will be a coach tour to a different part of the island, and we shall visit a spice plantation, then stay for two nights in a chalet on a coral beach, before returning home.

I've been thinking about this holiday, now that it will soon be over. There were days when I felt that I was learning about the people here and about their history, but I know that I've not been very brave, I haven't been much of an explorer!

I should like to have travelled more, but there has always been someone to look after, someone to care for, and I think it becomes harder when one is older, and on one's own.

But I have this record, and I shall read and think about it all again in the years to come. The island is the most beautiful place that I have ever visited or could imagine, though sometimes it is mysterious, even frightening.

And of course I hope that one day I shall be able to come back, and rediscover all those things that I have found here, and other things too perhaps, and understand them more completely.

January 2008

She leans against the landing wall, waiting for the agony to pass, her lungs empty and rasping as if she were breathing the thin-stretched air of the desert, or saturated thickets of jungle. At last she turns at the doorway of the bedroom and fumbles with the lamp; but something strikes at her heart, and she slips, falling hard and heavy against the bed. She does not move.

Her eyes are filled with brilliant colour, scarlet, gold, and crimson: she hears a sound of water, and the air is warm, and fresh, it lifts her — and she is sailing now, sailing on a fine wind, sailing, sailing to Zanzibar ....

On the shore, the men are gathering to prepare the evening meal, and dark-skinned boys run and laugh along the harbour wall. There is a scent of wood-smoke, and of spices, and the sun burns its pathway downwards through the sky, spinning, to the surface of the sea.

White Hyacinths

During those first strange, unsettled months, I passed the house almost every day, visiting my father at Rowan Court, or shopping in town for my own small flat not far away. Seeing the old place then gave me the sense of a past still present, still significant, which reassured me at that time of change.

The house stands at a corner, and the date of its construction, 1908, is marked on the front wall, above the door. It is a dark-bricked building with narrow windows and tall turrets, fantastic somehow amongst those dull suburban streets. Looking at it again after all this time, as an outsider, a passer-by, it's hard to believe that we lived there, as a family, behind that gloomy façade, all those years ago — more than forty years ago now. It was our home until I was almost seven, when we moved to a nicer neighbourhood elsewhere, but I have only a few faint memories of it. There is a mismatch between what I see now and what I can remember, as if I were looking at a snapshot taken with double exposure, the later shape superimposed upon the earlier one.

My mother died suddenly when I was only six, but I can remember very little of that sad time, and almost nothing of her, however hard I try. My early childhood is a place from which I am somehow exiled. My father's sister, Ellen, came to stay with us not long after my mother's death, to look after my father and me. He never remarried; I believe that was unusual, but there were many bereaved families in those years after the war, and neighbours were kinder then perhaps, and helped one another.

"It's strange, Dad — I pass the old place now, on my way here."

It was a Saturday morning, and we were making coffee together in the little kitchen at Rowan Court which visitors may use when they wish. It was one of those days that are winter and spring by turn. March sunshine polished the windows, the cups and teaspoons, and outside, crocuses in neat tubs along the terrace were like fragments of rainbow fallen there in the earth. In the shade, a few last traces of snow were melting, and beyond the terrace and the tubs a gardener was turning the hardened soil, opening it to the sharp air.

"Do you remember, Dad — Wiltshire Drive, on the corner there?"

I spoke slowly, very carefully, for I was not sure how he felt about those early years. "It's darker than I remember it," I added. "It isn't how

I thought of it, it's not the picture I had in my mind, somehow."

He didn't reply immediately, and I glanced towards him, thinking that he might not wish to talk about the place. He has never spoken to me of my mother, even now — that may seem unusual too, but he comes from a generation of men that did not speak of their feelings.

"Wiltshire Drive! You've been up there again, Esther?" he answered at last. For a moment he looked beyond me, as if his memories were painted along the wall, or scattered in the garden, and he could search out the past there. His eyes are dark, almost black, the whites very bright. Then he smiled a little — when he does this, one side of his face, the mouth, the eyebrow, slants more steeply than the other. It gives him a rakish air; I think it is irresistible even now.

"It didn't get the light, that house," he spoke emphatically. "Not any time of day. Never worked out how they managed it!" The smile climbed the side of his face again. "But after the war, everyone was looking for family homes, young couples like us, people made the best of things. We were happy there, your mother and me, starting out ..." The sentence faded, he concentrated for a moment on pouring milk, his hands not quite steady.

That morning he was dressed smartly as ever in his favourite navy blazer, grey flannels. A handsome man still, I thought, white-haired and straight-backed, though one leg was wounded during the war, and he uses a stick to walk. It is only his hands that seem old, as if age has touched them first, like an autumn frost at the edges of the garden.

"Even so," he continued after a few moments, stirring coffee, adding his customary one-and-a-half spoons of sugar, "I was pleased when we moved to Stanhope Close, it was a better area." He considered for a moment. "*Unsequestered.* Your Aunt Ellen liked it there too." He likes to use an occasional complicated word, taken perhaps from a newspaper, or from the crossword.

Auntie Ellen stayed with us until I left school, then she returned to her cottage in Lincolnshire. She is a smaller version of Dad, her smile slopes a little too. I believe they have always been very close.

"Unsequestered is very good, Dad," I said, and I touched his sleeve.

My father lived alone until last year, but when his eyesight began to fail, and he suffered one or two bad falls, I helped him move to Rowan Court, and I think it was a relief to him, though of course he would not say so. Soon after this, my husband Chris was offered a new post, opening a branch of his firm here in the town, and he will start in a few months' time. Our children are grown-up now, mostly away from home, and we are both happy to leave London. So I am searching for a house just as my parents did, all those years ago, and I can spend a little more time with Dad.

"You don't want to be wasting your time with an old villain like me!" he had protested, with his slantwise smile, lean chin jutting like the crescent moon; but I know that he is grateful.

I worry that I haven't been as close to him as I should, over the years. It was often lonely at home, and when I left school, I sometimes found reasons not to go back.

"We love having Laurie with us, Mrs Howard. He's settled in so well." Mrs Clark is the manager at Rowan Court, and recently, we reviewed Dad's first months there. We sat together in her tiny four-square office; a desk, some filing cabinets, and a hard chair are all the furniture she has there, as if she does not wish to take more space from her charges. But the sun finds every window here.

"He always has a joke for the staff, they do appreciate it. Some of our residents can always find something to complain about, but Laurie always seems to worry that he might be causing us trouble." She smiled, her pretty face plain with goodness.

Dad has always had a way with the ladies, but I don't believe it is intentional. It remains a part of him, though soon he will be eighty.

* * *

Memory is like a muscle, I think; when it is used again after a time, its energy returns. I glanced towards the house whenever I passed by, and some recollections came slowly back to me, superimposed on the vacuum that my early childhood seemed to be. I remembered making a fire in the grate in the living-room, clearing ash in the mornings. I could see the old coal-scuttle once more, its dull copper-black gleam, and the strange-shaped implements on their stand: the tongs, the shovel, the poker. The shock and fear of finding a frozen bird in the garden one winter morning came suddenly back to me, but still I could remember almost nothing of my mother. And after a time, I hardly looked towards the house as I passed, so I am not sure when it was that I noticed the 'House for Sale' board, and, in due course, another: 'Sold'.

Then the overgrown hedge at the front was cut down, and I could see the little triangular garden that was once so pretty — it must have been my mother who made it so. There are one or two old photographs that show her standing proudly before a slope of daffodils, or struggling with an old-fashioned mower, dressed in baggy land-girl trousers and headscarf. But the garden was neglected now, and sad.

Gradually the fabric of the house was stripped, turned out on to the thin grass. Cupboards, wooden mantelpieces and threadbare carpets lay there for everyone to see. Workmen arrived: ladders, buckets, tarpaulins, and over the next few weeks I saw men on the roof, men fitting windows, plastering and painting.

I couldn't resist the wish I had then to see inside. One morning, dressed a little more smartly than usual, I walked slowly by the house, ostentatiously looking. It was a fine day, though no light reached here, the buildings too tall for the narrow street. In my pocket I had an old picture of myself as a little girl, with my mother — how pretty she was, even through the grey-brown mist of the old photograph! She had wide-set eyes and a wide mouth; there was deep shadow beneath the points of her jaw, and she looked frail, too thin. We stood together on the front step, and she was smiling to me, slightly stooping, holding out her arms. The date of the house above the door proved the location.

As I stood before the gate, a tall man in suit and tie emerged from the door. "Looking for someone?" There was authority in his voice, I thought, perhaps money.

"Oh — I'm so sorry!" I exclaimed, as if surprised. "It's just — well — I used to live here — when I was a little girl. Our family lived here. Could I look inside, just for a moment? Would that be possible?" I touched the photograph in my pocket, but it was not needed.

"Well of course, why not?" he said, and he seemed intrigued. "I'm the owner now, I'll show you round myself. Just give me a moment, will you, I'm almost finished here."

The front door was scraped rough, ready for repainting. I waited outside, looking at the dreary yards and neglected gardens along the street, and I wondered, too late, if it might be a mistake to go back so far into the past.

But everything inside was stripped away of course, and I could make out nothing of the corners and contours of my childhood. The owner was friendly and understanding, however, and I told him a little about my father, and our family, and we exchanged our details.

When I left the house, clouds dragged along the roofs, releasing rain. In the wasted garden, a few white hyacinths stood, flowering alone by the gate, all that there was of freshness and fragrance in that bleak place. Somehow they had survived the neglect of the years, the flattening boards and planks. They seemed contradictory to me. Their colour was plain and pure, but the scent was very sweet in the rain, and heavy, like some rich drink. I stooped to touch the softly-clustered flowers and the sharp blades of the leaves, and I thought of my mother, the picture I had of her in my pocket. I wondered if it was she who planted them, how long they might last. Each year they would reappear, whatever happened about them, a witness, a memorial; the ivory blossom unfolding from the complex coiled bulb beneath the heavy earth, its long, deep-twisting roots.

Afterwards, I wondered if I had imagined them. When I passed by there again, a week later, I could no longer see them. Perhaps they had died away, or the workmen had crushed them. Perhaps the new owner had made different plans for his garden.

* * *

A few days later I received a package in the post, containing a short letter from the owner I had met that day at Wiltshire Drive. Another smaller envelope was enclosed.

Dear Mrs. Howard

It was a pleasure to meet you recently, and I hope that you are continuing to settle down here.

As you may have noticed, the renovations on your former family home have continued satisfactorily, and the property will be sold or let in due course. As often happens, certain items came to light when the old wooden mantelpiece in the main upstairs bedroom was stripped away. The papers must have been placed there at some time, then slipped down in the small gap between the mantelpiece and the wall, where they would be almost irretrievable, even if not forgotten.

I have given them only the briefest of glances, as they are obviously of a personal nature, but from the names on the documents, I assume that they belong in your family. I hope they are of interest or significance to you.

With kind regards.

James Fellowes

In the second envelope I found a few old postcards, an airmail letter from a distant cousin, hardly even a name to me; some receipts. At the bottom, an old crumpled sheet of paper.

And I was not prepared for the shock that I received then.

'Oh my dearest,' I read. 'I am so sorry, but I do not know how I can go on. I am not well, and I'm *becoming a burden to you, Laurie, I'm holding you back perhaps, causing you worry and unhappiness. I'm not able to be a good mother to Esther, and in this house I feel very much alone. Please forgive me, dearest Laurie -'*

It was written in pencil, fading and smudged, hard to read, on a single lined sheet of paper, an unpleasant yellow now. There was no date, no signature.

I sat heavily on a stool in the hallway, and the note fell from my fingers. Immediately my thoughts were back in the old house, in Wiltshire Drive. My early memories of it, and my recent visit, scraped uncomfortably in my mind again, not fitting together.

Could it be possible ...? Oh, surely, no, this was only something that she scribbled, lonely and unhappy one day, then slipped behind the mantelpiece, hearing him come into the house?

Slowly, I stooped to retrieve the note. The words were uneven, sloping through the lines of the cheap paper, as if they had been written with deep emotion. I leant against the banister, my thoughts shooting in my mind like fireworks in a yard, out of control.

Would he have known, before ...? Or did he see the note after her death and slip it himself behind the mantelpiece? As if he couldn't bring himself to destroy this document, this witness? And then later it fell behind some shelf of his mind — it was too big a thing for him, he couldn't speak about it ...

And I did not know. They had said my mother had heart disease, and I hadn't questioned this. In those days, that diagnosis might have meant a number of things. Conditions which today are simply and quickly cured could be fatal then.

My mind stumbled about this note and its meaning. I could not visit my father that day.

* * *

When I saw him again I told him about my visit to the house, and I spoke more casually and carefully even than before. We sat in the comfortable lounge by the French windows, looking out to the garden, where red and yellow tulips stiffly patrolled the borders. Some of the residents were enjoying the sunshine, their old faces lifted to its warmth as if to a friend, touching the plants with their fingertips. Perhaps already they felt themselves to be a part of this world, a world of leaves and wind-filled trees and gentle air.

"They've made some changes up there now, Dad," I said quietly, feeling my way again. "They stripped the old mantelpieces down, they even found a few papers behind them — old letters and things. They asked me if I would like to have them." I studied his face, the expressive white eyebrows, the fine features waiting for the smile that would set everything aslant. How handsome they had been, in those old wedding photos taken during the war! — Dad in his soldier's uniform, my mother so young. How happy: how untried.

There was no movement in his features, he showed no concern, no distress, though with one hand he pulled at the cuff below the other sleeve.

"Lord yes! I remember how things used to get down there. There was a fine old crack behind those mantelpieces, Esther, they weren't well-fitted at all," he said, not looking at me, but before him, into the garden, reflecting. "Not *contiguous*," he ventured. He waved to one of his friends there, past and present mingling in his mind. "Postcards and such, you put them on the ledge to deal with later, next day they'd be gone. You'd not get anything out from there."

"I like contiguous, Dad," I muttered automatically. "I wondered — would you like to see the papers, if ...?" I added.

He did not answer, though his fingers plucked at the cuff again. We drank our tea, and he pointed out to me a tiny, sweet-faced lady who would soon be ninety — she had been telling him about some of her early memories.

"Do you know, Esther," he exclaimed, "when Ivy was born, World War was declared!" His eyes were dark and bright with humour and interest, the smile cracked his face.

"Yes," he added, looking at his new friends, at their white heads, their bright brave smiles, their failing bodies. "Some of them here have a tale to tell!"

I looked at the pleasant scene in front of me, at the well-upholstered lounge and the well-tended garden, the elderly folk happy and cared for. I looked at the visitors, friends and families, grandchildren on best behaviour, someone's feathery flop-eared dog. I saw my mother coming as a white ghost through the door, her note in her hand. I saw my father, looking away from her, joking with Ivy, finding a clever word.

I thought of all that these old people might have done during their lives, what burdens of guilt they might still feel, bent by their pasts.

* * *

The following week Dad celebrated his eightieth birthday, and Rowan Court arranged a tea party for him, with a cake and candles. They were gathered in the comfortable lounge, all his new friends. There was laughter, as there is always here, it is a habit, a fabric that holds them together.

On these days of celebration, residents may be allowed a small glass of sherry or wine, and that and the occasion itself were too much for him, he became slightly confused. I took him to his room where he lay on his bed for some time, though he did not seem to be sleeping. He started to mutter a little to himself, and his fingers were shaking, stretched to mine as if seeking reassurance. I did not know quite what to do then.

"... you're a good daughter to me, Esther," he murmured. "I ... "

" — Dad ..."

Slowly his face became more relaxed, and he rested for a while. I saw him more clearly in that moment, I realised how frail he was; the frost was spreading. And I realised how frail he had always been, beneath the brightness. Perhaps there is always one moment when you see your parent not even as an equal, but as a child.

I sat in the chair in the neat, colourful room, thinking how little we know about the things that matter. I felt weightless, floating in memories and uncertainties. I longed like a girl for my husband Chris, for the warmth of his arms, his deep voice. We had spoken on the phone the previous evening, and as the conversation neared its end, I struggled to tell him, as if it were an afterthought, some of the things that were in my mind.

"Something Dad said, Chris — he and my mother, it made me wonder if things were always all right between them ..."

"Esther, love ... your mother died — was it forty years ago?" The receiver seemed to jump with the strength of his voice, and I pressed it closer to me. I realised once more how much I missed him. "Laurie's always worried about doing the right thing. You're just the same. Look, I'll be down in a few days, we'll make a decision on one of those houses — and we'll go out and celebrate, the three of us."

My childhood was a lonely one. I know my mother only from photographs; I search for feelings that are beyond or beneath memory, slipped too far down, to some dark dry place. I know that she died too young, and that sometimes she was unhappy — but in those days, many women like my mother were unfulfilled and isolated with their babies in dreary homes, without the comforts and aids and the medical care that we take for granted now. There was no counselling, no therapy.

I hadn't known what I might find when I visited the old house, and I learnt more than I expected; but I realised at last that my worries were foolish, and that I could put the past behind me.

* * *

I might have left my father then, but I was content to stay for a little longer, calmer than I had been for some days. I closed the window that looked on to the garden, for it was becoming cool in the early evening. The colours of the sky had become soft grey and pink, a coalescence so delicate that the brush of a bird's wing might break it.

I heard him murmur once more, as if to himself. His eyes were still closed, but his unsteady hand was stretched towards mine.

"I tried to do the right things ..."

"Of course you did, Dad ..."

"You can't always know what to do for the best. There isn't anybody to tell you." His voice had become a little squeaky, an old scratched gramophone record.

He was quiet for a moment. In the corridor unsteady footsteps passed by, a door closed.

"She ... we ... I didn't ... " he whispered, very faint, so that I could hardly hear him.

"Oh, Dad ..."

I bent to touch his hand again. I noticed the cuff was frayed there, where his fingers had pulled it.

"Don't, Dad," I said quietly. "Don't talk this way, there's no need."

The light was fading, but his eyes were wide open, fixed on mine. Or perhaps they looked beyond me, behind me, towards the garden, and the coming of darkness.

SHELLS

His old car was an intruder in the narrow, pretty street. He parked it as unobtrusively as he could, then stood for a few minutes outside the front door, searching in his pockets, slowly, one after the other, then through them again. At last he moved the borrowed key in the lock, testing it, right, left, finding which way it wanted to turn. He entered the hallway and let down his bag of tools and paints, but gently, so that the fine polished surface of the wooden floor might not be damaged. He seemed to fill the hall; a large man, over six feet tall, with legs like trees, and long feet confined within heavy, paint-streaked boots. The house around him was so small that he could almost lift it upon one hand, set it on his shoulder and take it where he wished, a stained Atlas bearing the world. He walked slowly through the rooms, careful where he trod with his big boots, careful not to sweep any fragile object from its place to fall and break unnoticed, to be later crushed underfoot. He knew his own size and strength, knew many times over that he was clumsy.

There were two rooms at the top of the house to be completely redecorated. There had been a loft which now was to be a bedroom and bathroom, and other rooms throughout the three floors needed some painting or repairs also. The young lady had not made up her mind about everything yet. It was a beautiful house, one of many similar in this newly-fashionable area of London, of course, and in this street they were all rather alike. Narrow, pastel-painted outside; within, small rooms and corridors, unexpected corners and angles, pretty views. He touched the walls, the woodwork, the surfaces of the furniture with expert fingers. It was many years since he had done work of such quality, and he knew that it was a good chance for him.

The young lady had lovely taste; already she had bought some fine furniture, soft carpets. He could not help thinking it unusual that she should own such a house and choose to live in it alone, but he knew that these days girls worked for themselves, they bought their own houses and cars and lived their lives as they pleased. He admired them for it. He wondered what it was that she did for a living. She might be an actress perhaps, or a dancer, she was so lovely-looking, with delicate bones and pearl-white skin .... Like many big men, he felt drawn to things that were small, exquisite: opposite.

In the bedroom at the top of the house he saw the shells. He had not noticed them before. He bent over them, delighted by their shapes, like nothing else in nature that he knew of. They were contradictory — everyday things of course, yet rare and beautiful, so different from the odd, simple creatures that had existed within them; enclosed and secret, yet with that delicate opening .... His eyes followed the strange spirals, he touched them gently with the tips of his fingers. He picked one up, feeling, yet hardly feeling its lightness in his palm. Then he held it to his ear, hearing, like a whisper, the distant music of the sea.

* * *

They had stood a little awkwardly in the room at the top of the house; it was bare and oddly-shaped, with a sloping ceiling and rounded corners. Its small size forced the two of them closer together, and they were compelled to move back into themselves, so that they should not inadvertently touch.

From the window they could see roofs and chimneys, a cloudy sky.

"It looks like we're in for some rain," the girl suggested, conversationally, to release the tension between them, or to ease his awkwardness. The weather looked dull and threatening to her, but he saw silver-grey clouds like mountains, heavy, yet infinitely light. He said nothing, however, for nothing occurred to him that he could suitably say. He shifted his weight back to the other foot, folded his arms across his chest again.

She hurried to return to the safer, common ground of their transaction.

"So here I should like — somehow, if you can manage it ..." She turned back to him, a little unsure, yet never really doubting that what she wanted would be possible, and confident that he would agree to do it for her. "... I should like the ceiling and the upper part of the walls a sort of deep rose pink, and the lower part — from about here — to be white; with a white carpet ..."

His serious face lightened and widened, and he smiled down upon her, slowly. "That will be very unusual, if I may say so, Miss Richmond. I like to do something unusual." His arms uncrossed themselves again and hung down by his sides, as if pulled down by the weight of the hands.

Her smile returned his quickly. She was surprised and amused that he had understood her so completely, and she knew that he would do the work well for her. He had dark curly hair, beginning now, just a little, to recede from his face, with its boyish snub nose and long square jaw; there was too great a distance between the point of his nose and his solid chin. His face was high in colour, maybe he was fond of his beer — but the dark eyes were too old for his face, as if they looked from behind a clumsy mask. He was full of contradictions. As with many big people, his bearing and behaviour seemed to hold an apology for his size, and for the space he must take in others' lives, the light he must blot out.

She asked him, "When do you think you might be able to make a start? I have some guests coming next month." Privately, she did not want all the untidiness and inconvenience of work in progress for very long.

He searched carefully through his pockets, leaving a silence in the room; she noticed that he used movement where others used speech to fill a void. Eventually he pulled out an untidy diary, pieces of paper emerging from it at every angle. She saw a copy of the estimate he had sent her, the address laboriously printed at the top. He held the diary in one wide-spread hand and noted something in it with a stub of old pencil. He wrote slowly, and with his left hand, so that he appeared awkward, writing the wrong way round. Even right-handed, he would still have looked ungainly, as if writing were not an activity he was much accustomed to.

"Well, Miss," he said, "as you would like it done quite soon — shall we say in two weeks?" It was not wise to be too quick to start a job, or it might seem that there was no other work on hand. He did not have much other work on hand.

She smiled at him again. Her hair slipped in a smooth curve to her chin, emphasising the width of her face there.

"That's good! Two weeks then. I'll be out during the day but you can pick up my key from the neighbour ..." She was drawn to this big shy man, and reassured that she could trust the house and her belongings to him.

At the door she tried conversation again. "Goodbye then, Mr. — er, Mr. Smithson. I hope the rain holds off till you get home ..."

He appeared anxious to go. "That's all right, Miss," he said, not looking at her but beyond, along the road. "I take the weather as it comes ..."

The door closed behind him. Its deep red was warm, yet somehow astringent, and he could not think of the name for its colour.

* * *

"Dad! Is that you, Dad? You're back late!" Tired, he entered his cold, chaotic house — the lock was broken, no need to search for a key — the boys shouting around him as he entered, boisterous and bored, wanting to be entertained. They had been mostly alone since returning from school, two hours ago; now their life burst around him like loose gravel under a car tyre.

"Dad, will you come and play football with me?"

"Can we go to the cinema tonight? — *please!*"

His sons' eyes were bright and dark like his own. The boys had the same short nose and long square chin, and they were as he had been at that age, though he hardly remembered being young. When he looked at them it was as if he was looking at his own soul, untouched by life and time; his skin, before it had become a hard, almost impenetrable casing. In his love for his boys he felt their potential, and fear that it might fail; he felt a determination also that it should not, as far as he could help it. He sensed all the strangeness that creatures so similar must follow different lines to different destinies.

Gradually he quietened them, but they would give him no peace until he had played a football game with them for half an hour. He was too big to play the game well, but they kicked a ball at him, and he caught and retrieved it somehow.

At last he returned to the hall and found the day's post, a few brown envelopes, already trodden by the boys. The hall was large and dark, its walls streaked with damp, for it was overshadowed by the great tree that grew outside in the yard. He would not cut it down, for it was a fine lime, and in summer the leaves smelt very sweet. He was seeing his home anew these days. For a week now he had been working and living in a different world, a world of success and charm. His own house was no longer a mere unnoticed extension of his own inner life, its walls the walls of his own mind; he saw its neglect, its shabbiness, with surprise and pain. Carrying the envelopes he went through to the kitchen, where he prepared a simple supper for them all, eggs, toast, tea — he rarely touched any stronger drink — such as he had prepared almost every evening for years, since Mary had left them. He no longer had to look for the bread, the eggs, his hands found them of themselves, cooked them, conveyed them to the table.

Outside the kitchen window, in the small back garden, hidden from the street, his few precious roses faded under the darkening sky. He had planted them for Mary, but when they flowered at last, she was already gone, tired out by the younger boys, and by Charlie and his needs, the endless needs of the disabled. Her fair hair was grey by then, her features lined and losing their coherence.

His neighbour, Joan, came down into the kitchen, and they had a cup of tea together at the table. She was a widow, living on the same street, her own children grown and gone away, time empty on her hands. Sometimes she would give the boys their tea when they came home from school, and often she sat with Charlie in the evenings, so that when he returned from work, he could have a little time to himself, and with the younger boys.

He lingered over the paper. Politics was of no interest to him these days, though reading at least delayed the hour when he must return to his own concerns. Then he cleared up the things, the unmatching plates, washed them, put them away. He called for the boys, who were playing in the yard, and when they appeared at last in the kitchen, he looked through their homework for a little, helping where he could, then took them up to bed. In the kitchen again he worked on some bills and correspondence until he was too tired to do more. Then at last, when he could delay no longer, he climbed the dark stairway, past the children's rooms on the first floor, to the top, where there were two rooms only.

"Is that you, Dad?" Only he could have interpreted the mangled words.

He went into the room where his eldest son lay, bent over the colourless twisted face, touched it a moment with his long fingers.

"How you doing, Charlie?" he murmured. All that there was between him and Charlie, a murmur and a mumble — all that there could be.

Joan sat patiently beside the bed and they spoke about Charlie for a few moments.

"Thank you, Joan," he said at last. "You get back home now, you'll be very tired." Then, as he always did, no matter how exhausted he was, he took the boy's soft hand in his own and talked quietly to him, of what he had done during the day, who he had seen, what his brothers were doing. Often in these evenings he would speak more than for days previously, of things he hardly knew he had done or noticed. Sometimes he wiped the boy's face, brought him something to eat or drink. He knew Charlie was hardly aware of his presence, but still he believed in this contact, and he would not let the boy go, to be lost in some grey institution, some dim corridor of welfare. Joan came every day, and there were other carers, but every night he sat here himself, though it drained him of his last energies. He saw clearly now how his life had narrowed to this tiny, lightless circle, apparently empty of all those things that turn a life into living, things he had forgotten about over the years since Mary left them.

He knew why Joan came. She was about his own age, or perhaps a little older; a tall, quiet woman, with shapeless legs, ankles spilling over her large flat shoes like dough over a pie dish, and large glasses that hid the wisdom and the warmth of her eyes. He knew she had a caring heart, a heart of gold, and it had occurred to him that he had a duty to the boys to give them another mother — perhaps even, by now, he had a duty to Joan. He must decide something soon, for everybody's sake.

At last he went to his own room across the corridor from Charlie. It was long after midnight. He opened the window, where darkness hid the ugliness of yard and street — he had given Charlie the better view — and he sat there for half an hour. He found some music on the radio, Chopin, he thought, and he watched the lines of sound curve against the sky. But the radio was an old one and sometimes the sound faded or became drowned by a shrill interference like the hissing of rain.

The other house was not so far away. In the darkness, the roofs and chimneys, the sky and the stars were the same.

He closed his eyes, and his thoughts turned like the music, his tired brain could not control them.

* * *

They lay in each other's arms on the bed in the little room, excited by a new passion. The bed-linen was soft pink and white, beautifully made; her nightdress lay on the floor beside the bed. They had brought the CD-player to the room — music and candlelight, an idea of romance. In the calmer pauses of love-making they considered the future, immediate and more distant.

"But when *is* all this going to be finished? It's taking bloody *weeks*. There's stuff all over the place still ..."

"Well ..." She hesitated, surprised. "He's doing it all so well ... There's a lot to finish, and he's doing extra things too, you know, things I didn't ask for, I just get home and find them done. Things you couldn't do ..." She laughed at him a little.

"I'm a lawyer, not a bloody odd-job man."

She turned away from him; her silky hair, colourless in the candlelight, lay over the pillow. She sometimes felt that David could be hard and arrogant, though he was the cleverest one of their year in the firm.

She thought of the man she had liked so much when they met (strange to realise it had only been that once); his clumsy arms crossed over his chest or hanging at his sides, his shyness, as he shifted his weight from foot to foot. She remembered the angular joints of his hands as they held the diary and manoeuvred the stubby pencil. She had not seen him since that time, but she had been conscious of his presence, of his big slow body moving through the house, amongst her things, his fingers moving along the walls, over their surfaces. They had spoken on the phone once or twice, discussing some point about the work. His voice was slow too, as if not much used.

"But David, I can't just ask him to go, just like that ..."

"Well, why not? Pay him for what he's done, or else give him a time-limit for the rest, speed him up a bit. Give him a kick up the backside. There can't be much more anyway, we could do it ourselves before I move in."

She turned towards him again. "I thought you didn't do odd jobs, darling ..."

Suddenly he was guffawing, they were both laughing.

"Kiss me ..."

* * *

And now she knew that she was lost, though she realised at the same time that she couldn't be very far from her home. She hardly knew how she had got there; she'd certainly not meant to come. The road was desolate, long and wide, and resembled a mouthful of broken teeth. The houses were all different, though alike in their ugliness and decay. From the outside they seemed empty of life, as if nothing worthwhile or pleasant could ever take place in them.

She knew his house as soon as she saw it. The front door was open, but all was dark inside. Before the house was an untidy yard, with weeds running in patternless lines here and there amidst the broken stones. The paintwork was old and grey, peeling from grey wood. There was one fine tree growing in the yard amid the desolation. She did not recognise which kind it was, and it took all the light from the house.

Stirred by a sharp evening wind in which there was the smell of rain, old newspapers blew along the gutters. One dirty sheet flew towards her, and a naked page three girl wrapped herself around her legs, so that for a time she could hardly walk. Two boys in leather jackets laughed and whistled at her from across the road, a mocking and hostile sound that brought fear to her stomach. She almost ran to the end of the street and was lucky to find a taxi. She fell, shaking, into its cushioned interior, almost rolling over on the capacious seat. She was laughing, but there were tears in her eyes.

* * *

In the bedroom his body filled the little wicker chair and stretched beyond and about it as if it were a child's. His eyes closed heavily, his eyelids dragged him downwards with their weight, and he covered his face to ease the pain in his forehead. His limbs ached. He knew that he must make a start, but he feared to make some mistake, or to fall and injure himself. All night he had sat up with Charlie, who had been restless and calling out across the landing, and he knew the boy called only for him. He could not bear to hear the sounds. He had gone to him, murmuring whatever came to mind, holding the ungainly body which was his own, that soon would be almost as large as his own, close to him in the darkness. It was not the first such night, and recently Charlie's wakefulness had become more frequent. He did not know how he could continue. His work demanded care and delicacy, mistakes could take many hours to repair. He needed to find new work, of good quality; he had hoped his efforts here would lead to something similar. He would never let Charlie go. The boy was — himself; another unsuccessful human being, another experiment in living gone awry, and his responsibility.

He had not seen the young lady, Miss Richmond, since that first day. Once or twice they had spoken on the phone, and her voice had been distant and sweet. But he had been working in her house, amongst her things, and her presence had always been there, hardly visible at the end of his mind. Now the work would soon be completed. Another few days perhaps, unless something else were found to be done; but he could think of nothing.

When the phone rang he picked up the receiver next to the chair without moving, and listened to her voice, to what it had to say to him. When it had finished he sat silent again. His long face became flushed and very dark.

He sat for a long time, motionless; at the window the clouds bellied towards rain. It was very quiet in the empty room, for no sound reached him from the street far below. He knew that all the rooms and corridors about him were empty also.

He noticed the most perfect of the shells as it lay there on the table, its pale pink, its incomprehensible pattern. He held it cupped in one palm, and the fingers of his other hand touched the smooth pearl, caressed it softly. It seemed to become warmer as he touched it, rosy, it became heavier in his hand. But his fingers were too clumsy, he could not find any way into its closed, mysterious heart. It fell from his hands and rolled away into a corner.

* * *

As he entered the house for the last time, rain began to fall outside; it hissed on the pavement and stung his face. He completed the last few tasks, then gathered his tools and brushes, cleaned them, and collected up the covering sheets. He moved methodically through the house, ensuring that all was tidy. The work was perfect, the colours delicate in shades of pink, white, a touch of beige, a deep red. Her lovely clothes already lay about the rooms again. He climbed the stairs.

In the bedroom he placed a few roses from his garden in a small vase by the bedside — he had not been able to resist the soft match of their petals with the colours of the room. It was the most beautiful work he had ever done, but now it was finished, it had ceased to be a part of him, and its intimate delicacy made him feel out of place. He wanted to go. He wanted to hear his sons' voices in the hallway as he entered his home, to sense Joan's quiet presence there; he wanted to touch Charlie's face as it twisted in its rare, spluttering laugh.

The flowers gave the room a warm, living fragrance; but the shells lay still on the table, pure and unyielding — very cold.

In the hallway he shouldered the heavy bag again, then he closed the narrow door behind him gently, but with relief, and went out into the street.

His Story

This is his story — Edward's story. Perhaps I should begin by describing how I came to meet Edward, but I do not at the moment know how I shall finish, for I do not know if Edward's story is yet finished, nor what it means. I hope that as I write this, its meaning will become clearer to me.

I think there are often one or two people in a group who do not speak a great deal. At school, there were boys who had their hands up in every class to answer a question, but one or two who always kept their eyes down. At college, I remember a student in my year who never spoke a word during seminars, yet at the end of his course he obtained brilliant marks for his work.

In our writing group, my theory was proven more markedly than ever. We came from different backgrounds, and had different aims, but we got on very well, and within a few weeks of the start of term we were sharing our work and our ideas about writing. Edward was the exception, however. He was perhaps the oldest of our group. He seemed to be retired, to live alone, though he wore a wedding ring. We assumed he was a widower, with a family grown-up and gone away, and after retirement, the leisure to pursue his interest. We all liked and respected him, though he said very little except when specifically called upon.

He was a man of what is often termed 'military bearing', and the straightness of his back, the right-angled nature of his shoulders were a fine, but alas, an unheeded example to the rest of us. He had a rich, pleasant voice, and a smile which made the tip of his nose turn upwards, and which summoned the little boy to his face, so that even in spite of the right-angles one could see him still a child of seven. His rare laugh was, I can only say, warm and delightful, and you wanted to laugh with him. His hair was thick and rather fair, and his eyes were extraordinarily powerful — a pale grey, with a darker rim, and when he turned them to you, it was an experience indeed. He had what I can only describe as magnetism, which we all felt, in spite of his habitual reserve. Even his silences drew you to him, as you questioned the reason for them, wondering what might be in his thoughts.

He was polite and considerate to us all, but he never attempted a closer relationship with any of us, and he came and went alone to the workshops, afterwards climbing somewhat stiffly into his small car and driving away.

I was a little closer to Edward than the others, I think, and literally so, because we lived not far from one another, and sometimes, if he saw me along the road, he would courteously offer me a lift. There were always books piled in his car, literature and poetry, religion and psychology and things. I live with my Mum; Dad left years ago. I felt comfortable with Edward, and I would have liked to invite him to visit us, but our house was always untidy, and when once I mentioned the possibility, he politely and with great charm replied: ' Thank you, Richard, that is most kind of you, but I have some things that I must finish this evening.' He always called me by my full name even though everyone else has always called me Richie. The full syllables and the way he pronounced them in his pleasant voice, together with his courtesy, made me feel as if I was, somehow, a greater person, one of his own stature and maturity, worthy of his fullest consideration. But in spite of this he left me at my own house and never invited me to his, nor engaged in any real conversation with me.

We circulated our work by email a few days before each class. When the week came for my first contribution, it was like — oh, it was like appearing to my friends in some strange new outfit. I remember that one evening Mum appeared in an amazing new dress, she was going out somewhere — I don't know who she was with, some of her colleagues from work I suppose — and it changed my view of her completely. Well, it was like that.

When Edward's turn came to submit a piece for discussion, it arrived at exactly the same time on every occasion. I wondered if he had been nervous that first evening. I had thought that he might write about historical events, something about war, or maybe a story with a professional or business background. Of course, I did not know what Edward's profession had been, we did not ask these questions in the group. We were writers, and equals in our writing.

This is part of his first piece. It was about a man who killed his own small son by mistake, driving from his house one morning. There had been a similar case in the papers at about that time, and we assumed at first that he had taken that as his starting point, and was describing the father's anguish.

I did not know — but how inadequate that phrase is — I could not know, I could not imagine that such a thing might happen, that it would be possible to destroy my son without the earth breaking open, the sky becoming dark. His small body lay there, his head crushed and bleeding, and there was no new sound, there was no change in the street, only the small usual movements of the morning.

And afterwards, when I saw one thing touch another, when I saw a finger touch a wall, a cup set upon a saucer, neither object affected by the other, each movement and each touch reversible, I saw the tyre crush the head, the blood flow on the stones, and nothing that could ever be changed or altered in any way ...

As you can see, it was powerful writing, imaginative, though I think we were all a little shocked by its subject matter. He remained quite impartial as we spoke about his writing, he exhibited no special feeling, but we felt from his manner that this was not after all an event he had imagined, but something he had experienced, though of course no-one felt that they could ask him. We looked forward to reading his future pieces, and we all wanted to help him find and refine his 'voice', as it is called. He had this effect upon us, though I am sure that he did not seek any such effect.

His second submission was a sort of ghost story, in which a woman in a pale nightdress haunts the writer every night, driving him mad from lack of sleep. Nothing original there, but the woman was pregnant. Here is part of it.

The nightdress was heavy and tight about her, so that she tore at it, she tried to snatch it from her body, she was swollen with the unborn child and she could stand no further weight upon her overstretched skin. The sounds of torn cloth were like the sounds of pain, of a creature torn by pain. When he ran from them, to escape them, they became louder, and harsher; when he turned towards them, to stop them, they were gone.

Her body was beautiful like the full round moon that slipped over the sky, until it was broken apart, shattered into scarlet fragments, and the red dust spilt through the universe ...

There was more of this stuff, I think we all found it rather embarrassing, especially from someone of his years, though we pretended otherwise, and earnestly studied the text, keeping our eyes down.

Some time after this, I experienced some trouble with my own work. I wanted to start upon a novel for my dissertation, but I could not find the right theme, nor the characters that I wished to live with, the setting that I felt I would like to research. It was a total case of Writer's Block. I suppose — oh, I haven't very much to write about yet, my life is still a bit of a mess really.

I began to think that there might be easier courses of study, and easier ways to pursue a career. We discussed it one evening in the bar, after a workshop. I won't write out all the dialogue, but here is a list of some of the reasons for wanting to write that we could think of between us:

"It's like moving the furniture, you can rearrange the world the way you want it." Samuel's parents came from Jamaica, and he has had a hard time in many ways, it was a struggle for him to get on the course. He works the hardest of all of us.

"Have a child, write a book, plant a tree — it's an old Arabic proverb," Megan said, *"three things everyone must aim to do before they die, to leave something behind."*

"There are seven narrative structures ..." someone pointed out, *"so you could try them all, try the same story in seven ways, exploring things technically ..."* But we all felt this would be very laborious.

"Writing the Wrongs, the Pen is Mightier than the Sword," said Hanno, who was brought up in East Germany. He has told us of some of the terrible things that happened there to writers and artists.

"You could explore a subject which is not well-known, take it as your background — like semiology, or tattooing."

"To record something before it passes for ever — a language perhaps, or a culture, a place ..."

Ideas were coming thick and fast, it was a really interesting discussion.

"To entertain, to tell a tale." Everyone agreed.

"To put something back," I said. I have always loved reading, it has been company for me, in a way. It would be good to create something of my own for others to enjoy.

But lying in bed that night I thought about Edward. I felt that none of these objectives fitted what we knew of him, although it crossed my mind that he might be exploring the seven narrative structures.

My theory was that he had some other purpose in his writing, but I did not know what it might be.

Edward's next submission seemed to be some sort of psychological thriller, different from the other stuff. This is the ending.

They visited each place, they searched the longest corridors, they climbed to the uppermost floors and to the lowest basements, but they could not find him. They heard insects scratch in the corners, they saw the water on the walls, and the blood on the floors, they smelt the stench of guilt, but they did not find the place where he was kept. They had kind words for him, strong arms to lift him, and warm clothes for his shoulders, but there was no trace of him.

It was melodramatic, but none of us touched upon this in our discussions, for again, we sensed that this was no mere flight of fancy. There was autobiography in it, we thought — but my theory is that it's always there, it's in what you choose to write about, and in how you decide to treat it. If I were to write about — oh, a Tibetan nun, or a Chinese cockle-picker, that is my choice and the words would still be my words.

I thought once that I might prefer to be a journalist. I felt that would give me the opportunity to write, but without the loneliness that writers experience, without the need to fill the page solely with the fruits of my own imagination, and realise their sad insignificance all too late. I did not always want to work alone, to be without the stimulus of a congenial environment and colleagues. With only myself and Mum at home, and of course she is at work all day, and sometimes busy in the evenings, I have been alone quite a lot since I was a boy.

Megan has already started upon the biography of a little-known woman traveller she has come across in her reading. She hopes next year to study non-fiction writing, and to develop the work for her dissertation.

"Because it's *true*, Richie," she said. "It's not just your imagination, it's about real things, real people, *facts*. Things that last, things that no-one can disagree with. It's *important*."

"But knowledge is always changing," I argued. "There's new stuff coming out all the time, science, history, everything, even ancient things, new techniques for finding out things. And in your biography how will you choose what to put in or leave out? It will depend on what you want to say about your lady traveller, and what you don't want to say, and that is just your view."

I continued: "Fiction is about *universal truths*, which are relevant to every place and every time, not about individual and particular facts."

I think she was about to ask me what universal truths I thought I was imparting in my work, but I quoted to her the start of Anna Karenina, where Tolstoy says that all happy families are alike, but all unhappy ones different. Though now I come to think of it, Mum and I are happy in our way, I suppose, but we aren't like the family over the road, Mother, Father, two children, cubs on Tuesday evenings, Sunday morning church. I'm sure they are very happy.

I think Mum is happy, I must ask her when I next see her, but of course I am never sure when that will be.

"What about the beginning of Pride and Prejudice?" Megan said. "*It is a truth universally acknowledged that a single man in possession of a good fortune must be in want of a wife,*" she quoted.

"Well, perhaps it was universal *there, at that time,*" I suggested.

Megan is very clever, but she will not let you forget it. I think maybe it is because she is small. Actually, I'm not particularly tall either. I was in an accident when I was ten, it was just after Dad left, and — oh, Mum was out somewhere, I suppose, and I ran out into the road. My left leg is a little shorter than the other one, it hurts a bit sometimes, but it's OK.

Megan is also beautiful, though she goes about like a tramp. I have never thought about this before, but maybe in some ways, life is difficult for people who are very beautiful, or handsome — and I wondered suddenly if that is true about Edward too.

It is strange, but I have never had these kinds of thoughts before. I think it is writing that encourages you to think about things, not the other way round.

Edward's last submission of the year was different again from the others. It was a long and rambling work which none of us understood at all.

I enter the Gallery, and I wander through the rooms. The walls are rich and sombre in colour — deep green, red, soft brown — and these are reflected in the pictures that hang upon them, so that I seem to be looking at paintings within paintings, and I can imagine that I might find myself somewhere in these pictures, portrayed on canvas, a figure in a crowd.

The frames around the pictures isolate them, as if they were memories. I stop by those that I wish to study, pass by others. I am searching for something particular, something half-recalled. Yes; it is here.

Its colours are plain, only brown and dull yellow, yet it is a picture about light, its source and direction, and its effect upon the surfaces it touches. This is almost all the movement, all the meaning. An old man, perhaps a scholar, sits at a table, his hand, frail and bony like a sea-shell, rests quietly there. The light pours from the tall window above him, patterning his face and forehead, it is strongest of all on the fabric of his cap and robe, turning them to gold.

There are things laid out upon the table — food, books perhaps, it is not clear — but his hand does not reach for them, it is motionless, indifferent.

In the centre of the picture is a great spiral staircase of rich wood, its steps worn with age. It twists on itself in wide curves, left and right, to the front and back, but always upwards, and its highest steps cannot be seen. At the bottom of the picture is a wooden frame, like the edge of a stage, as if the painter were reminding me that the picture is not real, that the stage might be entered.

At the right of the staircase, low down, I can just make out in the darkness a stooping figure, a servant, and he is tending a fire, the red points of the flames are small and sharp. I can see the long tool that he thrusts into them, and his peasant's face.

I feel the heat of the fire, I sense the stench of the servant's breath and I reel from his leering grin; I see the tranquil hand of the scholar and the serene light from his window.

Strange stuff indeed! We were not expecting a piece of art criticism, or whatever it was. Fortunately, we were short of time in our session by then, and our discussion was brief. I remember that Edward left us quickly that evening, gathering up his papers and leaving the room more abruptly than usual. I wondered if he felt disappointed by our reception of his work. At the door, he turned back for a moment and his eyes searched the room as if it was a picture that he wished to remember, almost as if — oh, as if he was still in the art gallery.

He called out "Goodnight, Richard, goodnight to you all. I regret that I have to hurry away this evening," with his usual courtesy.

And then, just before Easter, we learnt that Edward would not be coming back to us.

We were called together that evening, the whole group, and we were told that he was missing, after a boating accident. I remembered he had mentioned to me once that sailing was an activity he enjoyed, and occasionally there had been books on this, amongst all the others in his car.

It seemed a terrible thing, and we were utterly shocked, and very sad, for though none of us knew him well, his presence in the group had somehow been a focus for all of us. We had no heart for a workshop that evening, and gathered in the bar, where we sat quietly for a little, thinking of Edward.

Gradually, however, we became used to his absence from our sessions.

After a lecture or seminar, I would often walk the long way back towards my home — sometimes it seemed a bit empty when I got back at night if Mum was out — and I would pass the house that had been Edward's. Of course, there was no sign of life there, and eventually a sale board appeared. Then one evening — oh, it must have been May or early June — I saw someone standing in the street outside the neighbouring bungalow, a lady with her dog, and she was looking at both the places as if they meant something to her. I did not know if it was the right thing to do, but I spoke to her, introducing myself, and saying how sorry I had been to hear of Edward's accident.

"How did you come to meet Edward?" she asked, and we talked for a few moments. She told me that her elderly parents had lived in that bungalow for many years, a long time ago, they had been Edward's neighbours then. But she herself had heard only a very little about him and was not even sure if she remembered correctly. An 'unreliable narrator,' I reflected. But she did not think, from what she had heard of him, that he would have had an accident, for he was a skilled sailor. He had been a commander in the Navy, and he had sailed all over the world in all sorts of boats.

"Did you know Edward's family?" I asked her. She did not know much, only that he had been married.

"I met her once, his wife, quite a plain little thing, a few years older than him, I would think. I am not sure if there were any children." He had taken early retirement from the Navy, she told me, and then set up some sort of business for a short time. That was all she knew.

But what if the lady's parents had not remembered correctly? Were also unreliable narrators? I wondered.

Mum often says I'm unreliable, but she's not referring to my narrative techniques, of course. I reflected suddenly that perhaps we're all unreliable narrators, everyone, I mean.

And that is all there is about Edward, really, it is the end of his story. But I thought a lot about him. I felt that certainly he had been someone who might have made great things happen, or to whom great things might have happened. I wondered how someone so fine-looking, so — well — distinguished, whom everyone respected, could have left so little behind him — except for his writings, of course. It was as if — oh, as if that was all that he *wanted* to leave. Or maybe his writings were about someone else? But no, I am certain there was something *personal* in everything he wrote.

Megan sent me an email to apologise for the some of the things she said. We are going to go for a curry next week, and I am hoping to see more of her. She sent me another quote that she thought I might like, it's from Hamlet.

'And in this harsh world, draw thy breath in pain to tell my story.'

I stuck it on my PC; my theory is that it is relevant to Edward in some way.

Then suddenly, I realised that I could solve my own difficulties on the course by writing about Edward! I could examine his pieces and see if I could work out what his life was, or if I could find out about his life, maybe with some local cuttings, his war or business records, I could understand his writings. I could make something of his mysterious life by my own work, a *universal truth.*

Yes, I'm going to do it, even if I can't do it within this course, even if it doesn't fit in with anything, I know it is what I want to do. I don't know if it will be fiction, or non-fiction, or memoir or biography, I don't think it matters, it's all part of the same thing really.

But I want it to be about our group too, about different people who are all interested in writing, and about their lives, in Jamaica, Germany, everywhere, and how they came to write, what their writing means to them, the things we were talking about that evening in the bar, because Edward is part of that too. I want to understand it all. I want to leave something of importance behind me. Oh, and it will be about me and Mum too, I'm going to see more of Mum, and talk to her more, give her a hand occasionally. She must have been lonely often, and she works so hard for us both. Perhaps even she'll tell me about Dad, and what happened then. Now I'm with Megan, that seems important, somehow.

But mainly it will be about Edward. I may never know what he experienced. But I have been reading his last piece again, and I think he had found something that meant a lot to him. I don't understand it yet, but it was about the light in the picture, and the colour and the patterns it made on the fabric, it was to do with that.

And I think that is what writing is about too — about finding the threads and the patterns that are in peoples' lives, and weaving them together, making them into something really important, something great — oh, something that will last for ever.

Mum gave me another quote, it's from a play she went to the other night, by Chekhov, she said.

'We should show life neither as it is, nor as it ought to be, but as we see it in our dreams.'

I stuck the quote on my PC, together with all the others.

CELLO

Her window lay open still. She could see the squares of the panes, the sharp line of the sill that separated her from the long grey garden. Beyond, the neighbouring house, windows closed already, lights lit, thin screens against the coming darkness.

Shadows softened the outline of the old trees, the movement of the heavy leaves was settling. Moths fluttered amongst the branches with ragged wings, fragments of shadow. They slipped into her room, touching her cheek, the parchment of her hand, the thin irrelevant skin above the bones.

It was quiet, only the small movements of the evening. The sound was so soft that at first she hardly heard it, not knowing if it came from the room about her — the folding of linen, the murmur of a voice — or from the garden. Dead leaves perhaps, the first dead leaves of the season, turning along the path. Then she knew that someone was playing, though at first she could not recognise the music. She struggled to turn, so that she could hear it more clearly, almost as if she had been waiting. The sound was uneven, a little rough, with the roughness of bow upon string, uncertain and unskilled. For a moment the vibration seemed to fill her throat, her body, as if the sound were breath, or life itself ...

He walked before her slowly, amongst the twisted old trees of the river bank. She watched as he paused, standing at the water's edge, his hollowed face turned away from her, grey eyes looking far along the stream. She watched him all the time now, secretly, with fear, as if he were a stranger amongst them. Roots were torn up along the bank, branches cracked or bent, the strongest the most harshly broken, for recently there had been storms. The water was stained red with earth and leaves.

"You'll come with us Daddy, won't you?" the children had pleaded, and he would not disappoint them, though the November afternoon was prematurely dark, and it was hard for him to walk on the uneven ground. Already he was bent and stiff, moving painfully, looking downwards to place each step: an old man at forty, afraid to fall.

"Run and fetch your father back!" she called to the children; they were messengers between their parents. They stood on either side of him for a few moments, their narrow fingertips closed firmly within his square ones, as if even now they could draw strength from him.

"He'll be coming soon!" they panted, running back. "He said not to wait."

A huge winter sun sank low and red amongst the trees, and she saw his outline against it. The branches laid their bars across him, enclosing and imprisoning him.

There were marks of colour, faint in the sky, she raised a finger to touch them before they were extinguished, and darkness slid towards her from the horizon. A slight breeze at the window stirred her thin hair, lifted the collar of her nightdress, perhaps testing if she were yet ready.

There had been another day, long before their marriage; an April morning, very still, yet everything seemed to be in motion. Clouds racing, light splashing amongst leaves, and the world full of light, more light than substance. They had climbed upwards for hours along a path that he had found.

"It's much too steep!" she complained, out of breath. "I can't go any further."

"But we've got to try!" he told her, "we've got to get as high as we can," and he helped her with a strong hand at her back, over fences or fallen branches in their path. His ancient corduroys were spattered with mud. He looked down as if everything he saw was his creation, his possession, clouds running, the sun scarlet and

silver in the stream; as if he could draw what he saw into his head, behind his gaze, and hold it there forever.

She heard the sound quite clearly now, and she could recognise the music. Its voice was firmer, its single line held every colour and harmony, as if it were an orchestra that played. All that was inadequate or unfitting had been discarded, leaving only what was pure and perfect, the music cast complete, not built note by note.

"John? ..." she called.

She stood outside the door, a glass of water in her hand; she heard him try the strings. He had bought the cello when he first became ill, though it was far beyond their means. It stood in their bedroom, the case always open. He could hardly lift it now, but she heard the start of the piece that he had worked upon so intently. It was severe, archaic even, but its slow grave lines were more mysterious than any modern work, its phrases seemed all questions, more questions than notes.

"John," she called again. "I'm here, John. Can I come in?"

She knew that the music was covered with his marks as he had tried to find what lay beyond the lines and bars that held its sounds to the page.

She hardly recognised those sounds now as he played. A few notes, out of tune, out of time, harsh-toned — then silence. She did not dare to break it, nor to enter the half-closed door, but stood for twenty minutes there, holding the glass, then turned away.

The little chess set that had stood by his bedside — she had carried it with her always. Now it stood at her own. It was the only thing of his she had still, for the cello had been sold by the children, or given away, she did not know which. The set was made of ivory, they had bought it together on holiday — he had been a fine player. The pieces stood imprisoned in their squares, their rows, yet ready to slant and sweep across the board, with moves of infinite freedom, infinite variation ...

... her hand too was ivory as she tried to touch the pieces, but she could no longer reach them, she could not even distinguish them now, she could not tell chair from table, window from sky, everything was dark about her. Voices called in the house, but she lay still, one hand fallen towards the floor, the coverlet slipped away. The music of the cello curved about her, enfolding her; it turned and circled in the corners of the room and in the long garden, it reached beyond the dark trees and above them, and its song filled the distant spaces of the sky.

Rain stirred the grass, clearing the dry leaves, the last traces of the long quiet day.